Summer of '99

J.L. Hyde

By J.L. Hyde:

Underground

Delta County

Summer of '99

J.L. Hyde

For the friends I made at Camp Batawagama – summers with you were the best of my life.

First paperback edition April 2022

Cover Design by Justine Gab

ISBN 978-0-578-29297-7 (paperback)

www.jlhyde.com

"Another secret of the universe: Sometimes pain was like a storm that came out of nowhere. The clearest summer could end in a downpour. Could end in lightning and thunder."

- *Benjamin Alire Sáen*

Prologue

August 20th, 1999

There's a sweet spot that occurs most summer mornings for the wildlife of Lake Timothy. The beautiful hour after the sun comes up, but before the people of Camp Shady Oaks descend upon the waterfront to disturb the peaceful morning rituals of the creatures that inhabit the area. The painted turtles sunbathe on waterlogged trees stuck in shallow waters. The whitetail deer stand on the banks and drink from the calm lake. The occasional bald eagle soars over the trees, searching for breakfast.

A man casually strolls down the gravel path to the waterfront; the same path he walks each summer morning. Today, he's preparing the grounds for the arrival of hundreds of parents who will pick up their beloved children after two weeks of fun in the wilderness. It marks the end of his eighth season as

Camp Director, out of the forty-one years the camp has been in operation. Eight years teaching today's youth about nature, survival skills, teamwork, and the value of friendship. He sips his hot coffee out of his favorite red mug and exhales slowly; he's done his job.

He's already checked the arts and crafts and creative writing buildings. He's done a sweep of the canteen, the mess hall, and the latrines. He walked past each of the cabins, which were silently filled with sleeping campers. Now, he'll check the dock and waterfront area to ensure nothing is out of order for the parents' arrival.

As he nears the end of the path, the serene summer morning at Lake Timothy turns to chaos in an instant. Lying before the man, at the edge of the water, partially submerged in the lake, are two bodies.

They are face down.

Blue.

Lifeless.

One

Then

The only excitement I've felt in my fourteen years that rivals this moment would be that sweet drive south on I-94 where the greatest mall on earth comes into view on my right, immediately followed by Six Flags Great America on my left. Whether we exit left or right, I know my afternoon is going to be filled with riding the Batman roller coaster until I lose my lunch in a domed trash can or drinking virgin strawberry daiquiris with my friends at The Rainforest Café in Gurnee Mills Mall. Once my disposable camera was developed, either option would give me bragging rights to the rest of the 8th grade for at least two weeks, until Audrey Polanski returned from yet another European vacation with her rich grandparents. She would casually bring a box of authentic Belgian chocolates to 2nd period – there isn't a boy in my class that can point out Belgium on a map, yet Audrey somehow becomes a superhero each time she brings those stupid chocolates. Now that I say it out loud, I realize the attention Audrey gets from those boys may have more to do with her requiring a real bra a full year before the rest of us and a little less to do with the fancy chocolates.

Today, however, is even greater than a trip down to Chicago. Today is the culmination of two years of begging and pleading. Two years of trying to convince my parents I'm mature enough to handle two weeks in the wilderness. Two years of casually mentioning that Kira Mooney's parents can't believe how many chores she does on her own after spending a few weeks at summer camp. It's not that my parents finally caved in. I'm en route to summer camp because mom left us and my big brother Matt got a job with the railroad so that leaves dad and I staring at four walls, which happens to be situated directly outside his parenting comfort zone. I don't care about the reason I finally won; I'm just happy I did.

"Dad, I know I saw the sign a few miles back. Large and wooden, just like they said it would be," I mention, holding the printed directions in my lap.

"I swear, ever since they gave you broads the right to vote, you think you know everything. Now hush: I know where I'm going."

Normally his chauvinistic jabs roll right off my shoulder because I've been hearing them all my life, but today is different. Today I have somewhere to be. Today is the first day of the rest of my life. I'll be surrounded by one hundred other campers from different towns who have no idea who I am, which means I can be anybody. *Today is important.*

"You're probably right, dad, but if you turn around and take that road, the map says we will drive right along the lake until we get to camp. You work so hard, and you deserve a peaceful lakeside drive."

There it is; the reluctant smile.

"Oh, Quinnie Q, where did you get those negotiating skills?" he slaps my knee lightly before pulling a U-turn on the gravel road, his Silverado kicking up rocks in response to the quick maneuver.

"Just don't call me that in front of anyone, dad," I request.

"Yes Quinn, my dear, you have my word."

His smile tells me I absolutely do *not* have his word.

Sure enough, three short minutes later we are staring at a faded oak sign signifying the turn for Camp Shady Oaks.

A slight *"hmph"* is his only acknowledgement that I was right. Five miles down the winding gravel road we go, with a stunning view of Lake Timothy to our left for the duration of the drive. I spot several cottages along the road with families outside, enjoying the mild northern Michigan summer. The houses slowly disappear as we complete the final mile of the gravel drive. The trees hang over the road so low, we are suddenly passing through a beautiful emerald tunnel. Dad slows for a doe on the side of the road, who quickly changes her mind and leaps back into the lush woods surrounding us. I check the time and note that we are still fifteen minutes early, even with the detour. I see him glance at the clock and nod at the same observation.

The road dead ends into the entrance for the camp. We pass under a weathered welcome marquee reading WELCOME TO SHADY OAKS, FUN BY THE LAKE SINCE 1958.

"For the amount they're charging, you'd think they could afford a new sign," dad huffs.

"You promised, dad, no complaining. I've been dreaming of this moment for years."

He looks in my direction and smirks. "Oh, calm down with the dramatics, you're not old enough to have done *anything* for years," he says as he reaches up and lightly grabs my nose with his thumb and pointer finger, an annoying gesture he's been doing as long as I can remember.

Although my only glimpse into what summer camp life might look like comes from 1980's horror films, the scene as we pull onto the property is exactly what I have been picturing since the day I watched Friday the 13th and decided camp life was for me. It may seem strange to have my ideal summer camp arrival stem from slasher films, but they always start out with teenagers laughing and swimming on a beautiful summer day, don't they?

We are one of the first to arrive as dad pulls his truck into an open spot in the grass next to the mess hall. Several adults are standing in line with clipboards outside the hall; I assume they are counselors. I cross my fingers that I'll be assigned to one of the younger women's cabins because surely, they'll understand how to have some fun.

"Hello there! Check-in doesn't start for another fifteen minutes, but I'd be happy to sneak you in so you can go pick out your bunk. You know what they say about the early bird," an attractive woman in her 30s with neon yellow shorts and a white tank top shouts as we exit the car, giving me a friendly wink.

"Yeah, the early bird drops his kid off and gets the hell out of here so he can beat traffic caused by the assholes who don't show up on time," my dad grunts as he grabs my suitcase out of the bed of the truck.

A male counselor behind her coughs to cover his laugh and walks away before he can be scolded. As usual, I immediately jump in to apologize for my father. I've gotten quite skilled into charming uptight adults with my sweet-as-honey personality, which makes them forget how offensive my dad is. Her demeanor slightly softens as I introduce myself and she scans the list for my name.

"Ahh, yes, right here! Quinn Harstead. You're in the thirteen and fourteen-year-old cabin, B-2. It's to the left of the latrines, down the path toward the waterfront. You're free to pick any bunk you'd like! Make yourself comfortable and be back at the mess hall by 5pm for the welcome night dinner. It is a pleasure to meet you both and welcome to Camp Shady Oaks."

I roll my eyes as dad kisses her hand before we depart down the path to the cabin. He is either an asshole or a ladies' man, no in-between. I see the woman blush as we turn to walk away.

"If you have any questions, Mr. Harstead, I'm just a phone call away!" she shouts, and dad waves back at her before giving me a victorious wink.

"Yuck," I declare as I hand my backpack over to dad, who is already carrying my pink suitcase in his other hand.

We pass a small brown cabin with B-3 painted on the side. There is a beautiful view of the lake through the windows of the cabin, and I grow increasingly excited as we continue down the trail, knowing the view from B-2 will be even better. A few more steps down a narrow dirt path and there it is: my first taste of freedom. For the next two weeks, I will be in this beautiful, brown shack with girls my age and not a parent in sight. I won't have to listen to dad endlessly complain about my brother Matt's horrible taste in music or how Holmgren finally pulled his head out of his ass long enough to bring the Lombardi Trophy back to Green Bay where it belongs. No, for the next two weeks, it will be nothing but fun in the sun, hikes in the woods, and s'mores by the campfire. I will finally make friends with girls from other towns so I can go back to my stupid little school and let them know that friendship with Quinn Harstead is in high demand. The next two weeks are going to change everything.

Dad kicks open the screen door to the cabin, and it squeaks so loud he flinches as he props it open for me to enter. "Well, I guess your babysitter won't have to worry about you kids sneaking out in the middle of the night."

"It's not a babysitter, dad. We have a counselor. She will probably be so cool, she'll sneak out with us," I boast as I grab my backpack from his hand and search for a bed to claim.

There are three sets of bunk beds and four single beds. Dad mumbles something under his breath about the literal nightmare of this many teenagers under one roof, but I ignore him and run through the pros and cons of each bed.

"Quinnie, I'm going to let you make your own decisions, I just want to remind you that you're a light sleeper and having someone moving around all night above or below you will probably keep you up. You're not used to sleeping with anyone else around, kid."

I consider the suggestion.

"I'm here to make friends, dad. Choosing a bunk means I automatically have a friend for the next two weeks."

There's a sadness in his smile, quickly replaced by eyes wide with forced optimism.

"Baby, you're going to make so many friends, they'll be fighting over who gets to share a bunk with you."

We share a warm side hug, and he hands me my light pink suitcase, which has seen better days. I struggle with the rusted zipper and pull out my folded stack of sheets, placing them on the bottom bunk of the bed closest to the window facing the lake. I nod, signifying my choice and he smiles before helping me stretch the fitted sheet around the crisp, crinkly twin mattress. After a few minutes of setting up my bedding, hanging my clothes in the cubby next to the bunk and taping my Spice Girls 8x10 picture to the left of the window, we sit on the bed next to each other in silence, his back hunched to avoid hitting his head on the box springs above.

"I know this year hasn't been easy on any of us, especially you. I'm so proud of you for keeping your chin up and I just know you're going to have the time of your life this summer," he says before kissing my forehead. "You march down to that office and ask to call me if you need anything at all, baby, *anything*."

"I won't need to, dad. I'm going to be having too much fun," I smile.

Our emotional goodbye is interrupted by the creaking springs of the screen door to the cabin. A woman in her mid-twenties with long, chestnut hair and tan legs greets us with a smile. *I've hit the counselor jackpot.*

"Showing up early? You're already my favorite! Quinn, I'm Sarah and I'll be your counselor for the next two weeks," she declares confidently, smiles at me, and reaches out to shake dad's hand. "You must be Mr. Harstead."

The anticipation of what dad is going to say in response to this stunning creature is sending my stomach into backflips. I'm going to go from her favorite to her least before I've even said a word.

"Pleasure to meet you, Sarah. I'm sure you're going to take great care of my Quinn on her first venture away from home," dad says, without any inappropriate undertones.

I can't hide my shock.

"She's in great hands, Mr. Harstead. She's going to have the best summer ever. Now, if you'll excuse me, I need to prepare for tonight's welcome party. It was such a pleasure meeting you both!"

Dad nods politely and waves goodbye as Sarah jogs back out the screen door, her ponytail bouncing behind her like a character from Baywatch.

I look up at dad, my relief palpable.

"What? She's barely of age, I'm not a *total* creep, Quinn," he says as he once again squeezes my nose and winks.

I have, in fact, seen dad flirt with women in their twenties on multiple occasions, so I have to believe he refrained today just for my sake. It's the most considerate thing he's done in years.

"Alright, kiddo, I'm not going to drag this out any longer. I'm less than two hours away if you need anything at all."

I choke back tears and I'm not sure why. Maybe I'm just overwhelmed that this is finally happening. Maybe I'm wondering what it would have been like if mom were here.

"Go beat the traffic, dad. I love you."

He faces me and places both hands on my shoulders, looking me directly in the eyes.

"Now, remember: If they try to get all you kids to drink cups of Kool-aid at the same time, *run.*"

I smile.

"It's not that kind of camp, dad."

Two

The next hour is spent awkwardly introducing myself to each girl that enters through the slamming screen door. I'm sitting on my bunk, pretending to flip through my Tiger Beat magazine and hoping I don't seem too weird. Much to my surprise, only two girls seem to have arrived at camp together. The rest are loners like me.

Most of the parents seem to like me, as they always do, and I'm not sure if that's going to help or hurt my chances of making friends. I was voted "Most Polite" at 8th grade graduation and it resulted in an entire afternoon of mockery from my classmates.

There are only two beds left: a single twin bed in the corner and the bunk above mine. It's like choosing teams for dodgeball all over again and, as usual, I'm sitting here in silence hoping I'm not chosen last. When the door opens again, I force myself to make eye contact and smile at the girl entering. She doesn't have a parent with her, which is odd, and seems to be struggling with her two suitcases so I hop up to help her. I grab one of the bags out of her hands, and notice her luggage is in worse shape than mine.

"I'm Quinn. There's a spot above me if you'd like it," I try my luck, while acting as nonchalant as humanly possible.

Her big hazel eyes scan the room before landing on the bunk I'm pointing to.

"Right by the window, we can wake up and see the lake!"

I like her already.

"I'm Jessie, by the way. Thanks for your help."

I help her unpack and make her bed and, miraculously, the conversation isn't awkward or forced at all. My heart soars at the thought of making a friend so quickly. Visions of walking to the mess hall and hiking trails together dance through my mind. I remember hearing Kira Mooney reminiscing about camp in third period this winter, and she said she didn't make any friends her first year and had to assemble her tent alone on her overnight trip. *Absolute nightmare* she summed it up to a group of classmates, who leaned over their desks to hang on her every word. This scenario has stressed me every moment since – before I even knew I was coming to Shady Oaks. I wouldn't know the first thing about assembling a tent. Worry no more; I have made my very own friend on our first day at camp.

I learn that Jessie is a year younger than me and attends school in Iron River, which is a little over an hour from my home in Gladstone. R.L. Stine is her favorite author and Liar Liar is her favorite movie. After asking about me, she shuts up and listens, unlike most girls I know. It's as if God created her just to be my friend.

A lighthearted debate over our favorite Spice Girl (Obviously, Posh is the only acceptable answer) is interrupted by the door being kicked open by a petite brunette donning Ray Bans. She turns towards the two girls who arrived together, gathered in the middle of the room and smiles. "What's up sluts, miss me? I can't believe this piece of shit door is still squeaking. Like, get it fixed, broke-asses."

"Cassie, as we discussed last year, we don't use that word. It's not a term of endearment," Sarah, our counselor, says as she enters the cabin behind the last-arriving camper.

"But you also preach about honesty all the time, and these girls right here? They are *honestly* sluts, Sarah," Cassie says with a wry smile, giving the girls an exaggerated wink. She doesn't wait for Sarah to respond as she snaps her fingers and shouts for a woman standing right outside the cabin door. "Roberta, *más rapido,* my suitcases aren't going to carry themselves."

A petite Hispanic woman is assisted by our counselor as she struggles with three oversized Tommy Hilfiger rolling cases. She quickly shuffles over to the empty bed Cassie is wordlessly pointing at and unzips the smallest suitcase, swiftly pulling out a set of crisp white sheets. I'm nearly ten feet away and I can tell they are more expensive than my entire bedding set back home. The aroma of high-end fabric softener hits me, and I don't think I've ever smelled something so lovely.

The other girls are stunned into silence, and I have a feeling that I'm the only one in the cabin who doesn't know who she is. She scans the room and lifts her sunglasses up as her gaze lands on me.

"You. You're new. Where do you go?" she asks.

"My name is Quinn, I go to Gladstone," I answer with as much confidence as I can muster. "I'll be a freshman in the fall." As if that gives me some sort of added credibility.

She looks to Jessie, smiles condescendingly, and returns her attention to me.

"Bunking with a thirteen-year-old? You've got a lot to learn."

Although there's barely any sunlight in the cabin due to the lush oak trees surrounding us, she puts her sunglasses back on and turns on her heels to march back to Roberta, who is fluffing her decorative pillows.

"Roberta, that's probably enough. I should take over, so we aren't here until midnight," she snaps as the woman apologizes and grabs her purse from the floor before turning to leave. Cassie doesn't thank her or acknowledge her departure in any way. I'm assuming this woman isn't her mother, as they bear no resemblance, but I've never really known anyone rich enough to have hired help. Cassie seems like a total bitch, but I must admit – I'm intrigued.

Sarah rounds up the ten of us in the center of the cabin to go over the night's agenda. We have about an hour of free time to explore the camp, and then we meet at the mess hall for the welcome party. Dinner will be served while the counselors and personnel introduce themselves and let us know what we'll be doing for the next two weeks. After dinner, we will all head down to the waterfront for the annual Shady Oaks summer kickoff bonfire, where we will make s'mores and maybe even hear a ghost story or two. I have to bite my cheeks to contain my excitement. I don't need another strike from Cassie for being too eager.

Jessie and I look around at our belongings before deciding that our disposable cameras are all we'll really need while exploring the camp. I grab my tube of strawberry banana Lip Smacker out of my front pocket and nervously apply it to my dry lips. My Aunt Betty says my lips are chapped because I'm dehydrated, but dad says he survived his entire childhood without drinking a glass of water, so I'll be just fine.

As we make our way up the path toward the center of camp, Jessie looks around and I can feel the paranoia radiate from her face. She's making sure Cassie isn't within earshot so she can fill me in. I'm certain of it.

"So here's the deal. Cassie's a real bitch," she starts.

"You don't say," I smile and nudge her with my elbow as we continue our walk, keeping our voices low.

"Her parents own Huntington's."

"What do you mean *own Huntington's*? Like all of them?" I ask in disbelief. There are at least eight of the superstores in the Upper Peninsula of Michigan where we live. Huntington's is like the extreme north version of Walmart.

"Yep. Cassie Huntington. Her grandpa started the business back in the sixties and now her dad and uncle run it. The whole family is filthy rich," Jessie explains. "I don't even know why Cassie comes here every year, surely there's some sort of rich kid camp in Traverse City she could be attending."

We walk in silence for a minute as I let it sink in that I'm sharing a cabin with an actual millionaire. I've never seen one in person, at least that I know of.

"Just stay on her good side or she will make the next two weeks a nightmare for you," she warns.

16

"I mean, she can't be *that* bad. Surely the counselors would put a stop to it," I say.

Jessie lets out a quick snort and shakes her head.

"Her parents donated the money for the new mess hall *and* the arts and crafts building. Nobody tells her shit."

Since mom left us, I've become cautiously optimistic of anything good that comes my way and this is exactly why. I knew coming to camp was too good to be true. My perfect summer is about to be ruined by the daughter of the idiot who dresses up in a striped jailbird costume during every commercial break on channel 6 and shouts *Why pay more when you can pay less? Come hunt for a deal at Huntington's, where the prices are so good, it should be illegal!*

Fantastic.

"Alright, these are the latrines. The left is for girls and right side is for boys."

"So, there could just be a group of boys peeing or showering right next to us at any time?" I ask, amazed that we are allowed within such close proximity. I'm also glad that dad didn't seem to notice.

Jessie looks at me and, at thirteen years old, she already has worry lines by her eyes when she smiles. I am so curious to know her story, but don't want to blow this possible friendship by being too nosy too quick.

"I mean, there's a concrete wall between us. It's not as scandalous as it sounds. They aren't peeking through holes in the shower wall like a dumb eighties movie."

"Porky's is *not* dumb. It's a classic," I counter.

After an exaggerated eye roll, we walk to the other side of the latrines, toward the A cabins, which happens to be the boys side. I glance at Jessie with mild panic. *Are we allowed over here?* As if reading my mind, she confirms that we are only heading toward the activity courts, just before the A cabins. Once we round the corner, I see a volleyball court, several tetherball poles, a set of swings and a few randomly scattered picnic tables. I snap a picture. There must be forty kids in the activity area, most of them look to be our age or a little older. The oldest kids allowed at camp are sixteen and they are easy to identify because they are all gathered on the picnic tables, far too cool to be doing anything else. There's a boombox in the middle of one of the tables, playing "Return of the Mack" and I scold myself for forgetting my CDs, although I don't listen to anything nearly cool enough to impress anyone here. Dad says if I listen to any more Chumbawamba, he's going to throw my entire stereo into Lake Michigan without a single regret.

I turn to ask Jessie what kind of music she likes, but before I can get any words out, I'm hit squarely in the head by a volleyball traveling at warp speed. It doesn't knock me off my feet, but I do keel over to catch my breath. I feel the heat traveling up my cheeks, both from pain and embarrassment. Jessie is rubbing my back and I'm relieved to know I'm not alone to deal with this mortifying situation. I slowly rise so she can help me assess the damage to my face when I reluctantly look around through small gaps in my fingers, which are spread out on my forehead. I can't believe it – the only kids who even noticed what happened to me are the four guys playing volleyball. Everyone else is simply going about their business, far too preoccupied to worry about the 8th grader who just nearly got decapitated. Although it still makes me want to die that anyone at all saw me get pegged in the dome on my first day of camp,

I could cry from the relief of not having the entire Shady Oaks roster witness the incident. A boy from the game leaves his spot at the net and is slowly jogging towards me to grab his ball.

We make eye contact, and the world stops. It's just like they describe it in romance novels. I thought that bullshit was just made up by Danielle Steele to sell paperbacks with shirtless cowboys on the cover. No, Ms. Steele was telling the truth – the minute I see him, nothing else in the world matters. With a light brown bowl-cut like Jonathan Taylor Thomas, his deep-set chocolate eyes focus on me as he approaches. A quick smile confirms that he also has JTT's dimples. I'm in trouble.

"Whoa, I am *so* sorry. Are you okay?"

He places his right hand on my shoulder and my entire body tingles; a sensation I've never felt in my life. The only time I've even been touched by a boy outside of my family was last year on the bus when Joey Jacques sat on my head and farted while his moronic friends cackled. It definitely did not feel anything like this.

"Oh, it's fine. It didn't hurt at all," I lie.

He now has both of his beautiful, olive hands on my shoulders.

"C'mon champ, you can be honest, it hurt a little," he winks.

Swoon.

"I'm Aiden. What's your name?"

I've forgotten my name.

"Her name is Quinn. Quinn Harstead. She's going to be a freshman at Gladstone," Jessie eagerly answers for me.

He squints his eyes discerningly at me.

"Quinn Harstead from Gladstone, how many fingers am I holding up?"

He wiggles two fingers in front of my eyes like a peace sign.

"Two," I nod, as if I have really answered a tough one.

Aiden's lips curl up into a smirk and his hands fall from my shoulders as he bends down to grab the ball, lying in the dirt before me.

"I'm no doctor, but I think you're going to be just fine," he says before jogging back to his friends, who look annoyed that the game has been on hold for the last two minutes.

I've heard summer love described in so many beautiful ways, but it never occurred to me that it could happen in my life. I briefly considered the possibility of cute boys at Shady Oaks, but never did I think one would ever talk to me, let alone stare deep in my eyes and touch my shoulders. I *still* cannot believe he touched my shoulders. What could possibly be more intimate than that?

"Well, you'll notice he didn't ask for *my* name," Jessie says, interrupting my daydream about bringing Aiden to my freshman homecoming dance – an act so bold, even the seniors would be talking.

"Who is he?" I ask.

"Honestly, I don't know. I don't remember seeing him last year," she responds, already looking around, ready to move on with our camp tour. "But he's standing with Vinny Brooks, so he might be a friend of his. Vinny is here every year."

I turn to casually look at the group of boys, itching the side of my head in a maneuver that will surely distract Aiden from the fact that I'm staring directly at him. The boy that he's talking to, the one I assume to be Vinny, is also good-looking but has a devious quality to him. I can't quite describe it, something about the way he's looking around with his hands in the front pockets of his oversized jean shorts. It's like he's looking for trouble, something my dad tells me all boys my age are doing, all of the time.

My concentration is broken by a group of girls to my right, slowly strolling in front of Aiden and his friends. The group is led by Cassie, followed by her two minions. She lowers her glasses with one hand and subtly waves with the other, before pulling her glasses back up and laughing with her friends. She is smooth. She is slick. She is seasoned. I, on the other hand, made my grand introduction by getting ball-smacked in the forehead with such velocity I forgot my own name.

Jessie rolls her eyes and wraps her right arm around mine.

"C'mon, I want to show you the canteen."

I try my best to forget the fact that Cassie Huntington is about to steal the only boy I've ever loved so that Jessie can show me where I'll be buying all the sugary snacks to drown my sorrows over the next two weeks.

"How much money do your parents usually put on your account?" I ask, standing before the chalkboard list of snacks and drinks made available for purchase each afternoon.

"I have fifteen dollars to spend," she says, staring forward at the price list.

"Well, that's perfect," I answer. "I guilted my dad into throwing forty on mine, so if we pool our money together, we can get whatever we want."

The look in her eyes tells me that she perfectly understands what I'm doing and appreciates it. I have no idea what her situation at home is, but I know she arrived without parents and hasn't mentioned anything about what life is like in Iron River other than jabbering about some pizza place that is supposed to be the best in the whole state. The Saloon in Gladstone is actually the best, but I'm not in the mood to argue. My life may not be perfect, but I have enough snack money to make sure we have a good time and I'm happy to share.

She points towards a few small cabins beyond the canteen and tells me that they are the arts and crafts, wood carving, and creative writing cabins. We will be assigned dates and times to visit by our counselor. After the very last cabin, I see some sort of small structure through the overgrown trees, but it appears dilapidated. Jessie catches me squinting for a better look.

"Those are outhouses. That's where all the campers had to go back when Shady Oaks first opened in the fifties, before the latrines were built. Beyond those are a few old cabins that have been abandoned for years. I've never been back there, but I heard they are super creepy."

"This sounds like the start of a scary movie," I say, still staring through the woods, barely making out the shape of the old cabins past the outhouses.

A loud whistle blows in the distance, followed by a man's voice shouting through a megaphone ALL CAMPERS REPORT TO THE MESS HALL, IT'S TIME FOR YOUR SHADY OAKS WELCOME DINNER!

"If they set a scary movie here, the audience would die of boredom," Jessie says.

"Oh, I'm sure *something* crazy has happened here. They just don't tell us because it would be bad for business."

"You watch too many movies, Quinn," Jessie tells me as she turns toward the mess hall behind us.

"Maybe so," I respond, before seeing something move in the woods past the outhouses. Either my mind is playing tricks on me or that volleyball *did* hit me harder than I thought. I rub my scalp where it hurts, shake my head, and follow Jessie to our first Shady Oaks dinner. Here's to a summer I'll never forget.

Three

Now

Brigadoon (noun)
: **a place that is idyllic, unaffected by time, or remote from reality**

I used to think that having free time would be the answer to my prayers. It's all I ever wanted. Now, when the vast possibilities of how I'm going to spend my day are ahead of me, I lie in bed until noon. Sometimes I just stare at the ceiling for hours. If I didn't have a staff of people in charge of making sure I *do* get out of bed, I'd probably stay here all day.

"Miss Harstead, it's time for breakfast," a sweet voice sings out as she nears the top of the stairs. She opens the door with a tray in her hands and a warm smile on her face.

24

"Well, if it isn't the loveliest woman I've ever known," I smile.

"So charming, you're starting to sound like your father who, by the way, proposed when he stopped by last week," she says with an exaggerated smile, comically raising her eyebrows.

"I hate to tell you Christy, but he has proposed to most of the county by this point. Not saying you're not special, you just need to know what you're up against."

Christy throws her head back and laughs hysterically as she sets the tray next to me in bed. That's always how she laughs: head back, eyes closed, hand over her heart. It reminds me of the videos they play at memorials. In fact, maybe I should try to capture a few videos of her laughing, for that exact reason.

I see it's oatmeal again, accompanied by orange juice and a bowl of fruit. I'd love a cup of coffee, but I'll just get it myself after breakfast. I will never get used to people waiting on me hand and foot; it's worlds away from how I was raised.

"Don't worry, I brought you your special after-breakfast treat," she winks as she pulls out a plastic ramekin containing two white pills.

"How did I survive before prescription drugs?" I ask.

"How did any of us?" she laughs.

She sits on the edge of my bed, in the spot left vacant by the white tray that is now in my lap. I've known her long enough to know that something is on her mind.

"Quinn. It sure would be good to see you get outside today."

There's sadness in her blue eyes, masked by the encouragement she's trying to give me. I know she wants what's best for me, but it doesn't mean I have to like it.

"You get paid good money. What's it to you if I leave this place or not?" I question as I swallow the pills, washing them down with the fresh squeezed orange juice.

"Because I care about you, that's why. Everyone needs a little fresh air and a change of scenery once in a while."

I smile weakly.

"For you, Christy, I'll think about it."

This appeases her enough to get back on her feet and turn to leave.

"Don't forget, my friend is stopping by this afternoon. Maybe we'll enjoy a drink outside, just for you."

Christy laughs.

"Maybe, Quinn. That sounds nice."

She leaves the door cracked and I hear her depart down the grand wooden stairs of my home: Brigadoon. My parents saw the movie together on their first date, so it's always meant a lot to me. The bigger issue here is that I live in a home large enough to require a name and I'm still not quite sure how it happened.

Just yesterday, I was cramped in my tiny room, listening to Matt snore across the hall and my dad blare his John Wayne movies in the living room. Now I live in an estate so large, I can't hear much of anything coming from the other rooms. It's nothing like the house I grew up in. Its white marble tile is sterile and impersonal. I have a staff that waits on me hand and foot because, at some point in my life, that became a necessity. Sure, I go out of my way to make sure they never feel like staff. I treat them like friends. They are paid well, and they do an excellent job of making sure I have everything I need. I cringe at the thought of referring to them as family because every place of employment I've had that advertised their team as being *like family* during my interview turned out to be one toxic hell hole after another.

My home is now in the middle of the woods. The Hiawatha National Forest, to be exact. The same woods I fell in love with during my first trip to Shady Oaks in 1997, which somehow still seems like yesterday. Two miles down a long and winding drive, gated and locked away from the rest of the world. Away from those who may not be supportive of the path I took to get here. Some say I capitalized on tragedy. Needless to say, I've made a few enemies on my path to Brigadoon.

Four

Then

A man wearing nylon shorts with an inseam so miniscule it gives me secondhand embarrassment is playing a trumpet at the entrance to the mess hall. It's so loud, I am concerned for my teenage eardrums as we pass by him.

"Is that some sort of welcome night thing?" I ask Jessie, wiggling both pointer fingers in my ears in an attempt to assess the damage.

"Sorry to say, it's every night. And every morning. And every meal."

What kind of torture have I signed myself up for?

"It would be a shame if someone hid that trumpet before reveille tomorrow morning," Aiden startles us as he sticks his head between ours and whispers loudly, before passing between, towards his friends.

28

"Abercrombie and Fitch," Jessie states.

I tilt my head in confusion.

"The cologne he's wearing. That's what it is."

I've only been to an Abercrombie store once; it was in a mall in Wisconsin. Dad was less-than-thrilled with the shirtless male employee working the door and asked if they were running some sort of teenage brothel before my face turned crimson and I bolted. However, I do distinctly remember the store smelling like a salty, masculine paradise before I rushed down the hall to JCPenney. I can picture Aiden gliding around the store, completely comfortable with his cologne purchase, looking like he belongs.

If dad finds out I've fallen in love my first year at summer camp, he'll never let me return. Hell, he might even demand a refund.

Jessie recognizes a group of girls from the eleven and twelve-year-old cabin; she must have stayed with them last year. She motions for me to come sit with them; I'm hesitant at first, but I notice that the entire dining hall is filled with tables of mixed-aged campers. Cassie's warning to not mix with the younger girls apparently only applies to bunks.

"Jessie! What is B-2 like? Are all the girls cool?"

The question comes from a freckle-faced pre-teen who is looking to Jessie like she's a rock star.

"It's so different from B-3, we all smoke cigarettes and drink wine coolers," Jessie replies as she takes a seat on the bench, leaving room for me on the end.

Freckles doesn't seem to get the joke until the two girls next to her laugh and roll their eyes.

"It looks just like B-3, guys. The only difference is, I've gotta spend the next two weeks with Cassie Bitchington," Jessie dramatically huffs.

"Cassie Huntington is in your cabin? No way. Good luck!" shouts a tiny blond on the opposite end of the table.

As if summoned, Cassie enters the mess hall with her clique; the two girls that I recognize from our cabin. She searches the room for a suitable spot.

Cassie apparently didn't get the memo that at fourteen, we are supposed to be going through an awkward phase. The rest of us have a varying array of acne, orthodontic gear, and horrible haircuts that our parents paid ten dollars for. Cassie has smooth, golden skin and a darker brunette version of Rachel's hairstyle from *Friends*. Every outfit she owns proudly displays a different brand name; most I have heard of but could never afford. She doesn't seem nervous or uncomfortable, even when walking into a crowded dining hall. I guess growing up with money gives you a level of confidence I will never understand.

An older man with dark, hairy legs and a strong resemblance to Robin Williams blows a whistle and yells "GRUB!" and all the campers are on their feet before I can ask any questions. We all stand in line, first grabbing our trays and then quickly moving past several windows with dining hall employees behind them, serving different dishes. I wish I knew what the rest of the windows contained before I committed to chicken nuggets at window one, but I know I'll learn the ropes soon enough and won't always be panic choosing my dinners.

At the very end of the line is a dessert table and I smile as I grab a Rice Krispie Treat; they are mom's favorite.

I smell Aiden next to me before I see him.

"Avoid the chocolate cake, the guys told me that Marge always licks her fingers when she's making the batter," he says, so close to my ear that I can feel the warmth of his breath and my arms fill with goosebumps. I smile and search for something witty to say in response, but when I turn to him, he's already walking back to his table.

That's twice he has purposely made conversation with me. Not Cassie Huntington. Not any other girl in the mess hall. Me. Well, I guess it's not exactly conversation if he doesn't wait around for my response, but it still feels good.

Throughout the remainder of dinner, we are formally introduced to the head of the entire camp (the man with the hairy legs), the music director (the man with the deafening trumpet), the arts and crafts director (a lovely gray-haired woman who looks exactly like she *would* be the arts and crafts director), and the rest of the instructors, counselors, nurses, and mess hall staff. I giggle to myself as I identify the woman who must be Marge-who-licks-her-fingers. Everyone seems friendly, apart from the janitorial staff. It's comprised of two middle-aged men who barely look up when their names are announced. One has a mop and is already cleaning the floors where we all stood in line for food and the other has a wrench in his hand and a scowl on his face.

All the activities we will participate in are discussed: a swim test to determine which level class we'll be in, arts and crafts, kayaking, hikes, folk dancing (which terrifies me), and the famous overnight trips. All the cabins have one night in which they will pack food and supplies and hike to a remote destination to set up camp for the night. Every legend of Shady Oaks, every unbelievable story, every crazy shenanigan that I've ever heard has occurred on an overnight.

"Overnights are what separates the men from the boys!" shouts a male counselor with his fist in the air, who is immediately slapped in the arm by Sarah. I'm not sure what that phrase even means, but the way he smiles at Sarah after she reprimands him makes me uncomfortable. I hope she doesn't have a boyfriend; she doesn't need any distractions while she leads us on the best summer of our lives.

Captain Hairy Legs concludes the announcements by telling us where to put our dirty dishes and reminding us that littering anywhere on camp property is grounds for discipline.

"Remember, we are on borrowed land. Nature lives here. The animals live here. We are simply visitors and need to respect the land as if we are in somebody's home."

This is met by blank stares and a few eye rolls, mostly by Cassie and her crew. That little snot is most definitely going to litter sometime in the next two weeks and I will be right there, turning her in with zero remorse.

"Now, let's all head down to the waterfront, where we will have the opening night ceremony and might even be visited by the ghost of Timothy!" Hairy Legs shouts, his eyes wide and fingers wiggling, as if this will really drive home the spookiness factor. A few more eye rolls by the campers and we are all on our feet, cleaning up our plates and filing out of the mess hall.

"Timothy, as in Lake Timothy?" I ask Jessie as we exit the hall for our golden hour walk down to the waterfront.

"Nobody really knows why it's named Lake Timothy, so the adults like to make us believe there's some lost soul wandering around camp. It's pretty tame, compared to the stories the older campers tell. Just wait."

We stroll past our cabin, and I desperately want to run inside and grab a piece of gum while spritzing myself with body spray in case Aiden sits near us at the waterfront. Nobody else seems to be stopping in their cabins, and I'm not sure what the rules are, so I stay in line knowing that my breath most definitely smells like chicken nuggets.

The sun is setting over the lake as we gather in groups, waiting for instructions. The loudmouth (that is most likely Sarah's boyfriend) shouts for us all to find our counselors and take a seat in front of them. There are rows of wooden benches situated in a semi-circle facing the lake. We quickly spot Sarah a few rows down from the guy making the announcement and I see Aiden and his friends take a seat in front of him. My opinion about him and Sarah quickly changes when I realize that a romance between the two counselors could mean that our cabins may spend some quality time together.

I am overjoyed when Jessie takes a seat in the last row before the boy's section starts, directly in front of Aiden and his friends. I pretend not to notice him and smile as I point out all the sights at the waterfront and ask Jessie questions as a distraction. She tells me that the main dock is where the swimming assessments will take place tomorrow morning. The kayaks and canoes can only be taken out with permission. The scuba gear is for the campers who test out of the highest swim skills test – they get to ride the pontoon out to a small island in the middle of the lake where they will dive and explore with their tanks and masks. It's instantly my life's goal to pass all the levels and take that victorious ride out to the island.

I'm so lost in my visions of becoming Shady Oak's premiere scuba diving queen, I don't even notice Cassie and her clique sit down on the other side of me. Directly in front of Aiden. My heart sinks. How in the world do I get this boy to fall in love with me while Cassie Huntington exists, right in front of him?

"I hear you guys are going to give us a run for our money at state this year, Cass," says Aiden's friend, the one I noticed earlier at the volleyball court.

"I don't care about football, Vinny, but I'm sure we won't have a problem beating Menominee," Cassie snorts.

"Ouch! That's my new school you're talking about," says Aiden.

Menominee. He goes to Menominee. That's an hour from where I live in Gladstone.

"And who are you?" asks Cassie with a wry smile.

Shit.

"I'm Aiden, Vinny's cousin. I just moved here from Florida. And I'll be playing quarterback for the team that beats Marquette this year."

"Two 'yoots,'" I say, chuckling under my breath.

"Excuse me?" asks Cassie.

My face is hot; I didn't expect anyone to hear me.

"Oh, sorry…two yoots. It's a line from My Cousin Vinny. I just thought it was funny that you have a cousin Vinny," I sheepishly nod to Aiden.

This is so dumb. I cannot believe I've inserted myself into this conversation. He's never going to want to associate with me again.

Aiden and Vinny erupt with laughter.

"Oh my god, Quinn, that's our favorite movie! We quote it all the time!" laughs Aiden.

He remembers my name.

I crack the coolest smile I can muster and turn back around to face the water. Quinn Harstead, cool and collected. Cracking jokes with cute boys. *No big deal.*

I can feel Cassie's gaze on me. She wants to know how he knows my name. She wants to know how I could possibly be smooth enough to hijack their football conversation and make these boys laugh like I'm a direct descendant of Adam Sandler himself. I turn toward Jessie and make more small talk until Hairy Legs grabs the megaphone.

He starts speaking about the history of the camp and the property that it's built on, but my mind is on Aiden and whether he's thinking about me. I'm barely paying attention until a gigantic bonfire is built on the beach in front of us and the counselors gather around it, mumbling some sort of chant. I notice Aiden and Vinny's counselor is missing from that group, but I don't want to draw attention by turning around to check if he's still sitting behind us.

I see that a few of the adults are trying not to laugh as they singsong their silly little words about Lake Timothy. They are holding hands now and hopping around the fire in a circle. Maybe my dad was right about this cult stuff. These people are strange with a capital S.

TIMOTHY, MAKE YOURSELF SEEN AND JOIN OUR CELEBRATION! TIMOTHY, JOIN US FOR THE BEST SUMMER EVER AT CAMP SHADY OAKS! WE CAN'T DO IT WITHOUT YOU, TIMOTHY!

Shrieks come from the younger cabins as a white flash comes barreling out of the woods.

"I'm here!" yells a male voice.

It's a person covered in a white sheet, with two eye holes cut out. I recognize the stupid, dorky sandals of the missing counselor sticking out underneath.

"Boogie oogie oogie!" he shouts.

Everyone erupts in laughter. Cassie and her friends are unimpressed.

"I swear, this gets dumber every year," she mumbles.

I wonder if rich kids are just permanently unimpressed. I steal a glance back at Aiden and Vinny. They are smiling and clapping. Hairy Legs stands up once more and grabs his megaphone.

"Thus concludes our welcome night festivities! Everyone head back to your cabins and get ready for lights out. Taps will play in thirty minutes. Don't let Timothy catch you outside your cabins after that!"

I wonder if the whole white-sheet-friendly-ghost charade is for the benefit of the younger campers who must be terrified of the rampant stories told about the real Timothy. I'm glad I'm old enough to know that ghosts aren't real.

The memory of the motion I saw in the woods earlier pops into my head uninvited.

Even if ghosts did exist, they wouldn't be just running around vacant cabins on a Sunday afternoon...*right?*

I shake my head and wonder how I am already falling for this paranormal nonsense on my first day at camp.

I jog slowly to catch up with Jessie and we then head to the cabin to grab our toothbrushes and tubs of Noxema before making our way to the latrines. We line up at the sinks to take our nightly pills; Flintstones vitamins for Jessie and I and capsules from a big orange bottle for Sarah. Seeing a prescription bottle with her name on it makes her seem so much older than us. I can't wait until I'm in my twenties.

Thirty minutes goes by quickly and I'm tucked into my bed, trying not to move too much on the crispy mattress and squeaky box springs as the sound of taps begins from somewhere in the center of camp. I know I complained about the trumpet player earlier at lunch, but this might be the most beautiful song I've ever heard. I feel completely at peace and drift off before the music stops.

Five

Now

I've lived in this house long enough to know which stairs creak when I make my way down to the first level. There is no silent place to step on a few of the stairs, so I grab onto the railing and skip five of them at once. My white socks slip on the bottom step, and I scramble to balance myself, avoiding a crash. I just want a cup of coffee without gaining the attention of Christy. Or Randall, the cook. Or Bruce, who keeps the place secure.

I aim my sights at the Keurig in the corner of the kitchen and swiftly open the cabinet, hoping I haven't forgotten which doors squeak. I grab down a Classic Roast pod and stick it in the machine, tiptoeing over to the fridge to retrieve my creamer.

"Quinn. You know damn well that caffeine triggers your anxiety, yet here we are again."

Shit.

"I know, Christy. But today, you see, today I am not feeling anxious. So, I don't think a little cup of Folgers is going to drive me off the deep end. I might even enjoy it outside, like you suggested," I reply, trying to butter her up enough to ignore her issues with my caffeine intake.

I glance at the clock above the stove.

"Jessie is stopping by at two today and I need to get some writing done. I'm going to take my laptop and this delicious cup of coffee on the back patio and kill some time until she gets here."

Christy smiles. I love when she gives in. It doesn't happen often.

"Stay off the internet, Quinn."

I nod my head and press brew on the coffee machine. I left my laptop charging in the office last night, but before I even finish the thought, Christy has retrieved it and a blank notebook, which she hands to me with a smile.

"Go write a best seller," she winks.

A few hours later, I'm back in the office staring at a blank Word document. I tried to work outside. I tried to enjoy the fresh air. I couldn't. My thoughts rapidly jumped from being watched by someone in the woods to being watched by a drone to being watched by the staff. These last few years, I'm always being watched.

At two o'clock on the dot, I hear Christy open the front door and greet Jessie. I'm happy for the distraction and I haven't seen her in weeks. In fact, she's the only person other than my dad and the staff that I've seen in months. She's like a comfort blanket.

Jessie enters the kitchen and opens her oversized backpack slightly to show me a bottle of Rosé and winks. She always knows what I need.

"We are going to sit out back, Christy. You can take the rest of the day off; I don't think I'll be needing anything."

Christy huffs.

"Oh, and just who do you think is going to bring you dinner?"

I smile.

"You know, there was a time where I made my own dinner. I understand how shocking that may be."

She shakes her head and walks out of the foyer.

"You really want to sit outside?" Jessie asks. "Are you feeling okay?"

I grab two wine glasses from the cabinet on our way to the patio doors.

"I'm feeling great," I lie.

"Feeling fine and thirty-nine?" Jessie asks with a smile as she pulls a corkscrew out of her bag and pops open the Rosé.

"Oh shit, that's this week, isn't it?"

She cocks her head to the side in the same manner my mother used to do when I'd lie and say Mrs. Anderson didn't give us any calculus homework.

"Quinn, it's tomorrow. Your birthday is tomorrow. I'll let you fly under the radar again, but for your fortieth, we are going somewhere fun."

"Yeah, yeah," I mutter and sit in the padded patio chair, holding my empty glass toward her and that beautiful bottle.

I watch her as she pours my wine, and I know that something is on her mind. I've known her long enough to sense when she's mentally pumping herself up to start a conversation she doesn't wish to have.

"Spit it out, Jess."

She doesn't try to deny it. She simply pours herself a glass, sits in the chair next to mine, and pulls an envelope out of her bag.

"What's this?" I ask, accepting the envelope from her.

"Just read it."

There's a blue post-it on the outside of a folded piece of paper that says *Please share with Quinn, I no longer have her contact information.*

I nearly drop the paper. It's Aiden's handwriting. I haven't seen it in years, but I'd recognize it anywhere.

I unfold the paper to see it's a printed invitation. Aiden Brooks has purchased Shady Oaks and is reopening the camp this summer. The camp that has been shuttered and abandoned for twenty-three years. I knew Aiden had done well for himself, but I didn't know he had *purchase a summer camp* money.

The invite is for Memorial Day Weekend. Aiden has invited the "old crew" to come together for one long weekend before the camp reopens. According to the letter, all campers, counselors, and staff who attended Shady Oaks during the final two weeks of 1999 are invited. Well, those of us who survived.

"I think you should go, Quinn."

I stare at the letter a little longer.

Jessie takes a deep breath followed by a sip of wine.

"I have a very important conference that weekend, so I'm telling you now that I won't be able to go."

I quickly snap my head towards her.

"So, you're telling me I should go by myself? Are you nuts?"

"Quinn, there's a reason your books are bestsellers. People love your writing. Just because a few nuts tried to harass you afterwards doesn't mean they'll be there this weekend."

I give her a weak smile in anticipation of a question I don't want to ask.

"What about Aiden? We haven't talked in a long time."

Jessie smiles and shakes her head, reaching forward to tap the post-it note in my hand.

"He invited you back to camp, didn't he?"

Six

Then

By the third day of camp, I feel like I've been coming here for years. I navigate the grounds with confidence, I have secured my regular spot in the mess hall, and I know which shower heads have the best water pressure. Jessie and I are thick-as-thieves and I've managed to elude Cassie Huntington's attention for the most part. Life is good.

We are leaving the hall after lunch (Swedish meatballs; not nearly as gross as I expected) and I suggest we swing over to the canteen and splurge on a bag of Skittles and two cans of Pepsi to keep us entertained during the two hours of free time before arts and crafts begins. Jessie doesn't need much convincing; she loves sugar and knows I'll pay for it on my account.

Luckily, the wait at the canteen is short today. There are only two boys in front of us as we get in line. The midday summer sun is pounding on my back, and I consider that this may finally be the year I learn to put sunscreen on without my parents forcing me.

The first boy in line is asking entirely too many questions and I'm getting hot and irritated. I shift my weight from one foot to the other, as if this will give me some sort of relief from the discomfort. I just want to get our snacks and find a place in the shade to enjoy them.

"What are you guys going to get?" asks the boy in front of us, who I believe is in Aiden and Vinny's cabin.

He's not nearly as cute as either of the Brooks boys, but that doesn't seem to bother Jessie. The apples of her cheeks are slightly rosy as she details our sugar-filled afternoon plans.

"I'm Jessie, by the way. This is Quinn. We are in B-2."

He smiles and puts both hands in his pockets as he rocks back on his heels and replies, "Yeah, I know."

Jessie and I look to each other with amused confusion.

"One of the guys in my cabin has a crush on you, Quinn. I've heard all about you and your friend Jessie."

My heart drops like I'm at the top of the tallest roller coaster at Six Flags. I want to ask him if he's talking about Aiden and, just as I contemplate whether I should, he turns around and takes his turn at the canteen window. Jessie squeezes my arm, barely containing her excitement.

He finishes his order and turns to face us, a Dr. Pepper and pouch of Big-League Chew in his hands.

"I'm Jake, by the way. See you guys around," he says as he departs, but only directed to Jessie.

I wouldn't be surprised if she fainted right on the spot. She can't focus enough to step forward and place our order, so I give the canteen employee my account number and walk away with our Skittles, Pepsi, and also a Twix bar, just for good measure.

"He is so cute!" she nearly shouts as she takes one of the Pepsi cans out of my hand and pops it open.

"*So* cute!" I lie. She is glowing. This isn't the time for honesty.

"Let's grab paper and markers from the arts and crafts building so we can play M.A.S.H.!" she squeals.

I haven't played M.A.S.H. since seventh grade when Audrey Polanski clearly manipulated the results to indicate that I would end up living in a shack with Steve Urkel and nineteen kids while driving a van with no windows. For weeks, this stupid boy in my class named Josh would scoot his glasses up on his nose and shout "Did I do that?!" every time I walked in the classroom. I hate the game and refuse to believe it can give any sort of accurate glimpse into someone's future. Today however, I'll agree to play since it's just Jessie and I, and she promised we can find a picnic table in the shade.

I am in charge of keeping watch outside the building while she runs in to grab supplies. We don't think we'd get in any real trouble for borrowing some markers, but we'd rather not chance it this early in the summer.

"I'll be in and out," Jessie promises as she disappears into the tiny cedar cabin.

I turn away from the door and do my best *act casual* stance while I keep my eyes peeled for any adults. Immediately a screen door slams, and I swing around to scold Jessie for being so loud, only to see that Jessie isn't there. I hear the slamming noise once more and, as crazy as this sounds, I think it's coming from the abandoned area of the camp, just beyond the Arts and Crafts cabin. I can feel the hair on the back of my neck standing on end as I strain to detect any possible movement in the area, but there is none. From my angle, I can see two outhouses and one cabin, all with windows boarded up and weeds overgrown around the structures.

Jessie exits the cabin, tucking a few sheets of paper under her shirt and shoving two markers into her front pockets.

"What's the matter with you? You look like you've seen a ghost."

"Maybe I have, Jess. I swear someone was just in one of those abandoned buildings you were telling me about the other day," I say, pointing behind her.

"Hmm, maybe it was Dave, the Camp Director?"

I consider the possibility.

"Why would he be back there?" I ask.

"Remember how I told you the older kid's ghost stories about Timothy get a little intense? Most of them say that his spirit lives in the abandoned area of camp, still searching for his summer love, Susan," Jessie explains with an eye roll. "Maybe Dave caught some kids messing around over there, trying to scare each other. I'm sure it happens all the time."

"The old section of the camp is in plain view when you're over here. I'm surprised they wouldn't at least clean it up. All that overgrowth makes it look like an eyesore. Maybe they could even tear it all down and make more outdoor activity areas," I point out.

Jessie smiles.

"Well, the legend says that ole' Timmy wants the grounds left exactly how they are so that Susan can find her way back. He will terrorize anyone who tries to make changes."

"Are we really discussing the desires of a fictional ghost? C'mon, let's go play your game," I say, nudging Jessie toward the volleyball courts where there is an empty table luckily situated right under the shade of an old oak tree.

Thirty minutes later, we are both smiling at the sheets of paper in front of us, displaying the particulars of our future. Jessie is going to marry Jake (I may have cheated a little to make that happen), live in a houseboat with two kids and a Mercedes Benz. I am going to marry Aiden (although I would have settled for my second choice; Devon Sawa), live in a big house in the woods with no kids (score) and drive a shiny new Jeep. That sounds like the perfect life to me.

"Hide the papers!" Jessie says in a firm but hushed tone, her hand slapping the picnic tabletop between us.

I'm sure there is a counselor coming up behind me, so I gather the sheets of paper in one smooth swoop and crumple them up in my lap, hidden under the table. I then innocently look around above us, minding my business and enjoying the birdsong.

"Mind if we join you?"

I turn to see Aiden, Vinny, and Jake approaching the table. *Jesus.* That would have been worse than a counselor seeing the game. How would I explain to Aiden that all the shaded-in hearts around his name were just for the sake of a game and not because I'm some sort of obsessed weirdo?

"Hey guys," says Jessie and all three boys take a seat on the benches around us, with Aiden directly to my left.

We begin to make the most casual small talk that a table of thirteen and fourteen-year-olds can manage: school, sports, parents, and camp. Although my heart is nearly beating out of my chest, I turn to talk to Aiden directly.

"So, you moved here from Florida. Which part?" I ask, as if I know a damn thing about Florida other than the existence of Disney World.

"Right by the capital," he answers.

"Miami? Nice."

"Um, Tallahassee, actually," he smiles.

I am an idiot. Why do I even bother trying? I attempt to recover.

"I was just making sure you knew."

This thankfully gets a laugh out of him.

Our conversation is cut short by a high-pitched scream coming from the latrines. We all turn to look just as Cassie Huntington is tripping out the door of the women's side. Our counselor, Sarah, is running at full sprint from the mess hall toward her. Cassie appears to be hyperventilating.

Jessie and I head toward the commotion, the boys rising to their feet, but staying cautiously behind us.

"Cassie, slow down, what happened?" Sarah asks, gripping her shoulders with both hands.

"He was trying to watch me go to the bathroom, that pervert!" she screams.

Confusion washes over Sarah's face as she glances back to the latrines. Seconds later, one of the janitors exits the building with a mop in his hand. I now see that there are two large yellow WET FLOOR signs with a rope connecting them. Hanging from the rope is a handwritten sign that says, CLOSED FOR CLEANING. The rope is blocking the entryway into the bathrooms and the janitor has to step over it to exit.

"Excuse me, Miss Sarah, but this young lady entered the latrines when they were clearly closed for cleaning. I was mopping the showers when I heard someone in the restrooms and went to investigate. She should have never been in there," the man says, shaking his head and holding the dripping mop over the grass so it won't soak the path to the bathrooms.

"I should be able to use the restrooms whenever I have to go, without some creep barging in on me!" Cassie shouts.

"Okay, okay, let's all calm down there. There's obviously a little confusion surrounding the protocol when the restrooms are being cleaned. Cassie let's go back to the cabin and talk about it," Sarah says in a calm, monotone voice, attempting to soothe the irate teen.

"What, so I'm in trouble here? I'm in trouble and he gets to continue to get his kicks? You're sick!" she shouts in his direction.

The man seems to be using every fiber of his being not to scream back in return.

"Everyone, go back to what you were doing," Sarah instructs the dozens of us who are now gathered around the scene. She wraps her arm around Cassie's shoulder and leads her to the path back down to B-2. Cassie shakes it off and stomps ahead of Sarah, arms folded.

"We've got some high maintenance girls in Florida, but this one takes the cake," Aiden says to Vinny and Jake, who are now standing roughly five feet behind us.

I turn to him, shake my head, and shrug my shoulders. I further crumple the papers from M.A.S.H. in my hand and toss them into the waste basket outside the latrine building.

"Just so the rest of you girls know, the restrooms will be closed for five more minutes so I can finish cleaning. This will happen every afternoon around the same time, and I will *always* rope the door off, so you know it's closed," the janitor shouts to the crowd, before turning to reenter the building. He lets the door slam behind him and the loud clap echoes throughout the now-silent group of teenagers.

"Damn," mumbles Jessie.

"Agreed," I reply, and we briefly say goodbye to the boys before slowly walking up the trail to arts and crafts class in silence.

Seven

Now

Biscuits and gravy. The smell is wafting through the vents and directly into my room. Not a bad way to wake up. I tiptoe to my bathroom to splash some water on my face and throw a robe on over my pajamas. Biscuits and gravy mean that dad is here, and he will be the first to point out if I look tired. When he arrived last week for my birthday, he handed me a bouquet of flowers and immediately followed it with a comment about the bags under my eyes.

I splash my cheeks and pinch them a little to create a rosy glow. I gargle some mouthwash, throw on my favorite slippers and make my way down the stairs to start my day a few hours earlier than normal. Before

I'm halfway down, dad's voice bellows out of the kitchen.

"Quinn Harstead, get your ass out of that bed!"

I land at the bottom of the stairs and dramatically hold my arms out to announce my arrival.

"My sweet daughter is awake *and* ready for breakfast? Well, I take back half of what I said about you," he smiles, setting down a plate of bacon as he walks over and kisses the top of my head. Christy is sitting at the breakfast bar with a steaming cup of coffee and the clock on the oven tells me it's just shy of 7:30am.

"Why do you insist on making all this racket so early in the morning?" I ask with a sly smile.

"Early? I've already got half my day in," boasts dad.

He returns to his spot in front of the stove, and I look to Christy with my best *give me a break* eye roll, but she seems to have caught the unexplainably-happy-in-the-morning bug. *What is wrong with everyone?*

"Every morning is a good morning when Jim comes to cook," says Randall, coming in from the dining room. "I do love a morning off!"

"Agreed!" shouts Bruce from his office and I take a few steps back to peer in his doorway. He's sitting in front of his security monitors with a mouthful of bacon and an oversized glass of orange juice.

"Oh, so Jim Harstead stops by to make his famous breakfast, and everyone takes the morning off?" I ask, walking over to the coffee maker and reaching down my favorite mug from the cabinet.

"Quinnie, you know coffee makes your anxiety worse," dad says, nodding at the cup in my hand.

"Everyone's a doctor," I mumble as I set the mug down and grab a bag of decaf tea, holding it in the air to show the room before placing it into my mug. Dad gives me a wink and then sets his glass bowl of gravy on the island with a serving spoon.

"Okay, gravy and eggs are on the counter, biscuits and bacon are on the stove," he loudly proclaims. Everyone thanks him and waits for me to make my plate first. I laugh and hold out my hands for them to help themselves. I once again wonder when everyone's world started revolving around mine. I shudder when I think of how easily I've allowed this to happen.

Dad hangs behind with me as my assistant, my chef and my head of security fill up their plates. I watch him look at all three and shake his head with a weak smile; I know he's also wondering how my life has come to this. His independent little girl getting waited on hand and foot daily. He then grabs two plates and fills mine up: easy on the gravy, no eggs, extra bacon. He's the one man who *has* been making my plate for nearly four decades, only without the paycheck.

The staff all go their separate ways after filling their plates and dad leads the way into the dining room. I bring my hot tea and pull out one of the side chairs; the only time I don't sit at the head of the table is when dad is around.

We eat in silence for a few moments before he not-so-carefully breaches the subject of Shady Oaks.

"Well, I suppose you've heard by now that your little friend is stupid enough to reopen that camp."

I swallow my food and proceed with caution.

"Yes, I'm aware."

"He called the house last week."

I drop my fork.

"Excuse me? *Aiden?* Called the house?"

Dad's eyes are cold and unforgiving.

"Yeah, and you better believe I told that son of a bitch to lose our number."

"Dad, why would you do that?"

He slaps the table so hard I nearly choke on my tea.

"Quinn, half of the state was questioning if any of you kids had something to do with what happened and he left you high and dry to deal with it. I also have a sneaking suspicion he might be behind the harassment you received after the book came out."

Dad's hand is still flat on the table, and I place mine over it.

"Dad, he was a sixteen-year-old kid. He didn't know what to do. His parents moved back to Florida, and he didn't have a choice but to go with them. Also, I highly doubt he had anything to do with the threats I received. It's not in his nature. We just grew apart and our relationship didn't survive what happened that summer."

Our conversation is interrupted by the phone ringing. It's the house phone, which doesn't ring often. I'd normally let Christy answer it, but I'm right around the corner so I stand to grab the receiver.

"Good morning, Brigadoon," is the greeting I choose, which gives me an out if it's someone I don't want to deal with. I'll just pretend to be Christy.

"Hi, this is Samantha Miller from WLUC TV6. I was hoping to get a comment from Quinn Harstead about the reopening of Camp Shady Oaks this summer."

"How did you get this number?" I ask.

"Ms. Harstead, is that you? How do you feel about the camp reopening? Will you be making an appearance?"

I'm stunned. Everything for the house, including the phone lines, is listed under Brigadoon, LLC. Nobody knows I'm here. Or so I thought.

"Let me ask you again, how did you get this number?"

"Ms. Harstead, *Summer of '99* is what most fans consider to be the book that cemented your status as the Queen of True Crime. There is obviously a lot of interest surrounding the reopening and we are just looking for a statement from you for our coverage."

I quickly hang the phone back up, but my hand is shaking so badly I nearly miss. I turn around to face dad, who is still sitting at the table, looking to me for an explanation.

"That was TV6 asking for a statement. I didn't realize everyone knew the camp was reopening."

"Sweetheart, that property is ground zero for one of the biggest mysteries in northern Michigan's history. You can't be surprised when it attracts a little attention for reopening after all these years. Not to mention, this world has become obsessed with true crime stories. I wouldn't be surprised if Dateline showed up."

I can't believe this is happening. There are just too many emotions to process. I'm happy for Aiden and his success, but I worry that kids will enroll in camp just to live out some sick fantasy of being at the scene of the crime. I want to see him again, but the thought of facing everyone from that summer ties my stomach in knots.

"Alright, sweetheart, I'm going to throw these plates in the dishwasher and head out. Call me if you need anything and don't you even dream of going near that camp, young lady. Nothing good can come of it."

I don't care how old I am, I always shrink a little when being scolded by my father.

"Yes, sir," I answer before kissing his cheek goodbye.

Later that night, I quietly sneak into the office to find the little scrap of paper that Christy keeps the wi-fi password on. I don't go on the internet anymore, as my therapist determined that it was the root of my anxiety and a plethora of other mental health issues. After *Summer of '99* came out, the bulk of the hateful comments I received were online, so I hardly fought the people around me when they decided it was best that I logged off for a while. The actual threats to my life came in the form of letters in the mail, which is why I had to change my address and my daily routine. I haven't googled myself in years and I'm in a much better place because of it. If I need to research a subject for a book I'm writing, Christy normally sits next to me while I do.

God, she doesn't get paid nearly enough.

I find the piece of paper and type the password into my laptop's wi-fi settings. I click on my browser and the Google homepage appears. I am nauseated. Christy would kill me if she knew what I was doing.

I'm just going to check on the news coverage for the camp's reopening and that's it. I just want to see what the basic story is. In and out and back to bed. Easy as that.

I type *Camp Shady Oaks* into the search bar.

I nearly fall out of my chair as my screen comes to life with results. All the recent news articles are at the top of the page. I quickly scan the headlines.

Scene of 1999 Tragedy Gets New Life from a Familiar Face

Camp Shady Oaks to Reopen, 23 Years After Tragedy

Inside the Memorial Day Weekend Reunion for the Shady Oaks Survivors

Will Bestselling Author Quinn Harstead Return to the Scene of the Crime?

I click on the last article. It's from True Crime Digest.

Camp Shady Oaks, abandoned since 1999, is reopening to the public in June, twenty-three years after its abrupt closure. The property, located in Michigan's rustic Upper Peninsula, is the location of the area's most notorious unsolved case, recounted in Quinn Harstead's bestselling novel "Summer of '99." According to county records, Shady Oaks was purchased late last year by tech millionaire and former camp attendee Aiden Brooks.

In 2015, Summer of '99 was adapted into an Emmy-winning ten-part miniseries for HBO and launched Harstead into true crime superstardom. She has penned a total of eight bestselling accounts of small-town crime stories, three of which were adapted into award-winning television series after the success of her book about the mysterious Shady Oaks deaths. Notoriously private, Harstead took that privacy to a new level when she deleted all her social media accounts and essentially went off-the-grid nearly two years ago. Her representatives have not returned any calls or emails requesting comment.

According to multiple sources, Harstead and Aiden Brooks were teenage sweethearts at the time of the tragedies in 1999. The question that is on everyone's mind: Will the reclusive Ms. Harstead come out of hiding and make an appearance for the camp's reopening?

Eight

Then

Seeing Cassie's little clique circle around and console her as if there had been some sort of tragedy was a complete joke to me. The girl had urinated, in an enclosed stall, in the same room as a grown man for thirty seconds. He never came within five feet of her. She deserved an Academy Award for the performance she was giving. If you could have PTSD from sharing a bathroom with someone of the opposite sex, I'd need intense therapy for all the times my dumb brother Matt busted in to use the bathroom while I was trying to shower.

Jessie and I did our best to ignore the drama and focus on things that really mattered, like this afternoon's swim class. Luckily, we both were placed in the Level 4 group after taking our skills test. Level 5 is the highest, which means I'm right on track to test out of it and join the scuba group by the time I turn sixteen.

I've noticed that she continues to use the still-damp one-piece pink swimsuit from the previous day each time we dress for swim. I don't want to overstep, but I happened to pack four suits and we are pretty much the same size. I mention it as she rolls her suit in a dry towel, attempting to warm it as much as possible before putting it back on and jumping into the cool lake.

"I see you forgot to bring a second suit. I'll make you a deal: I'll lend you one of mine to alternate in with yours if you'll share your face wash with me. My Noxema tub is nearly empty, and dad said he didn't have time to take me to get more before we came," I looked at her, trying to meet her eyes and show I'm sincere. "Deal?"

I wasn't sure if she really saw through my charade, but she went with it anyway.

"Yeah, I can't believe I forgot my other suits. You got yourself a deal," she reaches out to shake my hand and then surprise attacks me with a snake bite on my forearm.

"Ouch!" I yell with a laugh. "Now I'm going to give you the swimsuit I've been farting in the most!" I blindly reach into my suitcase and grab the first one I find, tossing it towards her and running away before she can toss it back.

We arrive at the waterfront five minutes before swim lessons and, as Jessie drops the towel from her shoulders, I am overjoyed to see that my swimsuit fits her perfectly. Now I just need to find a tactful way to tell her that she can take it home with her, as I have a sneaking suspicion the suit she brought is the only one she owns.

Cassie and her followers (who I now know are named Rachel and Trishelle) arrive just as we are walking down the dock to greet our swim instructor, Lena. As luck would have it, our entire cabin ended up in Level 4, so the ten of us make up the 4pm daily class. I actually enjoy swimming right before dinner because I'm usually starving when we get done and will gladly feast on whatever Mess Hall Marge is serving up.

I turn to watch the girls walk down the dock and both girls are by Cassie's side, rubbing her shoulders the entire way. It takes every ounce of energy I have not to roll my eyes so hard they get stuck in the back of my head.

The next hour is spent perfecting our front, back, and side strokes. The water is so deep, we grab onto the wooden planks of the dock each time we complete our laps, until Lena announces that we all need to let go and work on treading water.

We each push away from the safety of the dock and begin kicking our scrawny little legs to stay afloat while she starts her timer.

It's amazing how much time you have to think about worst case scenarios when you are silently treading in murky lake water and don't know how far down the bottom might be. My mind is racing.

What if I were pulled under by weeds?
What if I were pulled under by Jason Vorhees?
What if I were pulled under by the ghost of Timothy?
What if I lose my endurance and give up, sinking to the bottom?

Jessie is right: I watch too many scary movies. My horrific daydreams are interrupted by Lena's whistle; our time is up. We all managed to tread for the full four minutes, with the exception of Cassie, who needed a minute to *collect herself*. Now that I look at her body dramatically thrown on the end of the dock like a fainting woman from a black and white movie, I register that this little demonstration is not because of her trauma, but to gain the attention of the fifteen and sixteen-year-old boys' cabin. All ten of them are nearly crashing into each other as they stare at Cassie's sun-kissed legs while kayaking on the other side of the dock.

"Miss Huntington, either hop back in the water or head up to the infirmary if you are too unwell to participate in today's swim lesson," Lena instructs, instantly turning back to face our group and not allowing Cassie the opportunity to run her mouth in response. *I like her.*

Cassie reluctantly gets back in the water and participates in the second tread session before class ends and we all head up to shower before dinner.

"You don't think anything more serious happened to her with that janitor, do you?" Jessie asks once we are far enough away from the rest of the group.

I furrow my brows and cock my head in her direction.

"Jess. C'mon. She's a drama queen. If that man laid a finger on her, she'd already have her father on the phone and everyone at this camp would be unemployed. She's just attention starved."

Jessie seems to consider my words and nods in agreement.

"You're probably right."

An hour later, I've showered and applied my strawberries and champagne body wash, lotion, and body spray – fully prepared to make Aiden swoon if I should encounter him at dinner. My hair is still wet as Jessie and I walk to the mess hall. A quiet girl from our cabin, Caroline, is walking just behind us. She seems to read books and keep to herself most of the time. She has thick, coke-bottle glasses that she removes for swim class, and I often wonder how terrifying it must be for her to swim without them. Jessie reads my mind as she slows to talk with her.

"Caroline, right? I'm Jessie and this is Quinn. You're welcome to sit with us anytime during meals."

Caroline scoots her glasses up with her pointer finger and smiles. She is holding her tattered Goosebumps book, which tells me she normally reads during meals instead of talking to other girls.

"Okay," she responds sheepishly with the hint of a smile.

Before we even reach the double doors to enter the mess hall, the aroma tells me that tonight's dinner is burgers and fries. *Score.* Hairy Legs is greeting each camper with an enthusiastic high five as they enter, and I chuckle to think of the colorful things my dad would have to say about this poor man.

We take our normal spots with Jessie's friends from last year and I scoot in to leave a spot for Caroline on the end. We introduce her to the group and her face turns ruby red as she awkwardly raises her palm in response, eyes never leaving the table. I can't believe I've finally met someone more awkward than I am.

While we are finishing our meals, the music director passes out songbooks so we can all follow along with the words of the cheesy camp anthems they force us to sing nightly. There is an entire song about Mountain Dew, and I must admit that it makes me smile because just about the whole camp laughs at the ridiculous lyrics when we sing it.

All the picnic tables in the dining hall are lined up back-to-back during meals. The music director explains that when the next song's instructions tell us to clap, we first clap our hands together and then the next time is with our "back yard" neighbor. We are to turn around and high five the person directly behind us, right hand first and then left. I secretly hope Cassie is sitting behind me so I can accidentally slap her forehead and blame it on my clumsy nature.

We begin the song, which is oddly about writing a letter home to our parents and telling them about how horrible camp is and how we want to come home.

Hello mother, *clap clap*

Hello father, *clap clap*

I turn to clap with my neighbor when instructed and my body freezes when I see that it's Aiden's cabin seated behind us. Vinny is directly behind me, and we clap hands. We are both smiling at the silliness of the song. Aiden is on the end of the bench, next to Vinny, so he's clapping hands with Caroline. If it isn't going to be me, thank God it's Caroline. She looks so uncomfortable. When we spin back around to face forward and finish the song, I nudge her a little and whisper about how fun this is. She smiles. The power of persuasion is a real thing.

I wish I never would have seen Aiden behind me, because that's all I can think about now. I do my best to act nonchalant as we all rise to dump our plates when Hairy Legs loudly announces the conclusion of dinner service. Aiden is next to me, and we are scraping our plates into the trash at the same time.

"Had I known Vinny would get to touch your hand, I would have taken his seat," he says before leaning in front of me to place his empty plate in the bus tub to my right.

"That would have been cool," I respond, impressed that I am able to form a coherent thought.

"You smell amazing," he says.

He stops for a beat and looks directly in my eyes and winks, smirking just enough for his dimples to show. What fourteen-year-old boy on this earth has enough confidence to wink at a girl? My knees are weak. Before I can speak, he's gone.

Nine

The day has finally come. Jessie, me, and the rest of the cabin are packing our bags for our overnight trip. According to Sarah, after we are packed and we stop at the kitchen to get our meals, we will be transported by van to an unknown location to begin our hike into the wilderness. We will build a fire, cook our own meals, assemble tents, and who knows what else. I cannot handle the anticipation; my cheeks hurt from smiling all morning. I throw my disposable camera in the side pouch of my backpack; I'm going to want to remember this.

"Gather round, ladies," announces Sarah. "I just got our trip information from the main office. We'll be staying at Shadow Lake."

Cheers erupt from half the cabin. The other half is smiling in response to the excitement from those who seem to know what Shadow Lake is. Judging by the rare positive reaction from Cassie and the minions, I think we've been assigned a good location.

66

"Those who have been to Shadow know that it's not an easy hike. But you girls are tough, and I know you can handle it. The reward will be jumping in the beautiful lake and sleeping under the stars. Let's go!" Sarah shouts, throwing her backpack on and slapping the wall over the screen door on her way out. Each of us follow and jump, attempting to do the same, yet none of us are quite tall enough to hit the spot. Maybe next year.

We march in line around the back of the mess hall, where there is a large cargo van with the back doors open, backed up to the kitchen doors. Marge is loading supplies into plastic crates on the ground outside the door. She looks up with a smile to greet us and I see one of her front teeth is gold-plated. There is a still-smoking cigarette half-stomped out by her right foot.

"Oh, you girls are going to have so much fun. I packed you the freshest meat we have for your hobo dinners," she tells us, her raspy voice indicating that the cigarette was definitely hers.

Sarah tells us to load the crates into the van and take our seats.

"Oh, and girls, watch out for the dogman!" Marge shouts, her cackle so loud and disturbing, it makes my skin crawl.

"What the hell is the dogman?" I hear Caroline mumble as she enters the van behind me.

"Some stupid urban legend," Jessie replies. "She's just trying to spook us."

"It's not an urban legend," responds Rachel, one of Cassie's crew. "My uncle saw him at his hunting camp ten years ago."

The entire clique nods in support of Rachel's hearsay account. There are four rows of padded benches in the van. Cassie turns around from the front row to face Jessie, Caroline, and me in the second.

"The dogman is absolutely real. He has the body of a man, but the face of a wolf. His howl sounds like a human and people have died of fright just from looking at him. He comes every ten years, and only in years ending in seven."

"How convenient for your little story that it's currently a year ending in seven," I say, looking past my fear of Cassie to give my new friend Caroline a little comfort.

The door slams as Sarah climbs into the front passenger seat and turns towards us to do a head count.

"Hey Sarah, according to the legend, when does the Michigan dogman come around?" Cassie asks.

"Oh, the dogman! I forgot about him. He only comes out during years ending in seven," Sarah answers and takes a moment to consider her words. "Well, 1997, sounds like we might be in luck!" Sarah opens her eyes wide and raises her brows a few times. Cassie turns back to us with a smug smile.

I can hear the other girls in the rows behind us whispering about the possibility of this creature's existence. Obviously, he *doesn't* exist. People just love a good story. I can't blame them.

I didn't notice until just now, but the man driving the van is the second janitor. He was announced at the welcome dinner, and I've seen him around camp doing odd jobs throughout the week. If he's friendly at all with the other janitor, I'm sure he's not too fond of Cassie Huntington. As if on cue, I catch his eyes in the rearview mirror and I swear he squints and glares straight at Cassie. Sarah announces that all ten campers are accounted for, and he puts the van in drive.

It takes approximately five minutes for my motion sickness to set in. I can hear my mother's voice in my head, telling me I should have asked to sit up front. What was I thinking, sitting in the second row of a stuffy van full of people?

"Any chance we could open some windows?" I ask, trying my best to face forward and keep my eyes on the horizon, like dad always tells me to do.

"Of course," Sarah answers. "Are you sick?"

"Trying not to be," I respond.

The trip takes twenty minutes and all twenty are spent bouncing along a pothole-ridden gravel road in the middle of the woods. I am taking deep breaths and willing myself not to vomit. I am continuously convincing myself that we are almost there. I've been looking forward to this overnight trip for as long as I can remember, and I don't want to waste a single minute with car sickness. Sarah repeatedly looks back to check on me and I swear it only makes me sicker. Cassie turns around and waves her hands in my face with an evil laugh. Just as I am considering asking the janitor (I now remember his name is Greg) to pull over, he miraculously stops the van on the side of a road. I have no time to question why we are stopped in the middle of nowhere as I push past Jessie and throw the side door of the van open. I drop to my knees as soon as I hit a patch of grass and begin to dry heave. I feel a hand on my back and a bottle of water appears in front of me. It's Sarah.

"She purposely tried to make me sick," I say, referring to Cassie.

"I know," Sarah responds, and I know she wants to say more. I cannot imagine how much her hands are tied due to Mr. Huntington's money and influence.

"Deep breaths, Quinn. Deep breaths. Take in the fresh air."

I listen to her and take a long inhale, opening my eyes to the woods in front of me. I can hear birds singing from the trees. A stray cloud momentarily blocks the sun from my eyes. The world is starting to steady itself.

"You're going to be a good mom someday," I say to Sarah, and she laughs.

"Fingers crossed it's not anytime soon," she responds with a wink. She hops to her feet and grabs the water bottle from the ground, handing it to me as I also rise. "Alright girls, gather round!" All the girls are already outside of the van, stretching and drinking out of their own canteens.

"There are ten of you and five crates. The trail is two miles long, so we will make it easy – the first five girls will carry a crate for the first mile and then hand it off to the empty-handed girls for the second mile. Everyone understand?"

Everyone nods in agreement, but nobody makes a move to grab anything. Thankful for her patience while I wasn't feeling well, I help Sarah by reaching forward to the crates to start the trend and four other girls quickly follow suit. It's not nearly as heavy as I expected. We all say goodbye to Greg, and he tells us that he will meet us at this exact spot tomorrow at noon. "Unless the dogman gets you," he adds with a crooked smile.

"Enough of this dogman bullshit," Jessie says as he drives away.

"Hey – language," Sarah says, trying to suppress a smirk.

I realize about a quarter mile in that this crate is a lot heavier than I thought. My hands feel like they are starting to blister from holding the handles and my shoulders are starting to ache from the straps of my backpack, which now has a tent attached to the top. My motion sickness is lingering, as it always does. The girls without tents on their bags have cooking equipment tied on, and the clanging of pots and pans with every step is making my head pound. I stay quiet and remind myself that there could be so many situations worse than the one I'm in. I've had to do that a lot this year.

I've never been so happy to hear Sarah's sweet voice when she announces that we are officially halfway in, and we can hand off the crates to the other girls. By luck, Cassie is behind me, so I turn and hand her the red plastic bin, overflowing with god-knows-what.

"Ew, sweat much?" she asks in disgust as she grabs the handles.

"Oh, just wait," I reply with a forced smile.

We begin the second half of our hike and I feel light as a feather. I am so glad I chose to carry the first mile. Now I can enjoy myself and all the nature around me. I place both of my hands under the straps of my backpack to take the pressure off my shoulders. It's Sunday, which means we've officially been at Shady Oaks for a week. Time has flown by.

"I'd give anything for a Big Mac," Jessie says from in front of me.

"Why did you have to say that?" I ask, now starving with a kind of ravenous hunger that only a Big

Mac could cure. I spend the rest of the walk thinking about how isolated we've been from the outside world. Sure, we've sent letters back and forth with our families (dad hasn't sent one yet, but I'm sure he will) but none of us has spoken to anyone outside of camp, listened to the radio, watched TV, or consumed any outside news at all. There could be a war going on for all we know.

A light appears through the thick cover of the trees, and I know there must be a clearing ahead.

"We're almost there, girls!" Sarah shouts from the front of the line.

One by one we make it to the campsite, which is simply an open spot in the middle of the woods with a fire pit dug in the center. There are ashes in the middle of the pit, and they look fresh. Another cabin must have camped here last night. We all drop our bags and collapse on top of them, gulping out of our canteens like we've been stuck in the desert for a week.

"Careful ladies, that water needs to last you until tomorrow at noon!" Sarah reminds us. "Let's get our tents set up while there is plenty of daylight, and then we can check out the lake. If anyone needs help with their tents, let me know."

I look to Jessie, and she mouths "I've got this."

Sarah pulls a small radio out of her bag and sets it up on a log next to the fire pit. She pulls the antenna up and soon enough; we have Jewel's latest single playing as the soundtrack for our tent assembly.

Jessie is a pro at this; she hands me the poles and gives me instructions like she does it for a living. Relief washes over my body as I watch her effortlessly drive the stakes into the hard ground. She's amazing.

I glance over at the other girls; everyone is working together to quickly assemble their sleeping spots, except for Cassie. She's sitting on a log, eating a Snackwells cookie and watching her friend Trishelle do all the work. Sarah takes a deep breath, ready to confront her, and thinks better of it.

Caroline has been paired up with another girl who arrived at camp alone, Samantha. They are working in silence, but getting the job done so I'm not worried too much about her. I've tried to keep an eye out for Caroline ever since she started sitting with us during meals. She seems like she could use a few good friends.

"Alright, tents are assembled, let's get our suits on and do some swimming!" shouts Sarah, clapping her hands together in excitement.

Within minutes, we are all running down the narrow trail to the waterfront to check out the infamous Shadow Lake.

It's better than I could have imagined. The water is a giant sheet of glass, not a ripple in sight. There is a sand beach big enough for us all to lay our towels out and kick off our shoes. Although there isn't a lake in northern Michigan that could be described as warm at any time during the year, this water is as close as we could hope for. As I walk in slowly up to my ankles, I think it may just be the first time I haven't felt a shock to my system from entering a lake around here.

"Ladies, look!" Sarah exclaims, pointing her finger towards the woods to our right.

There is a bald eagle perched in the tree and, as if on cue, takes off to seamlessly glide over us. I think of mom and how excited she gets every time we see an eagle. I used to roll my eyes as she would repeat how "majestic" it was every five seconds, but now I finally get it. It *is* majestic.

We all enter the water a little deeper, promising Sarah we won't go in over our heads. We spend the next hour playing keep away with an inflatable ball, doing handstands while our palms sink into the soft sand at the bottom of the lake, and seeing who can float on their backs the best. Unfortunately, the winner is Cassie, but she also has an indoor pool at home, so she gets a lot more practice than us commoners.

Sarah announces that it's time to get dressed and prep for dinner and she gets no argument out of us; we are all starving. The girls jump out of the water, barely stopping long enough to grab their towels and flip-flops before running back up the trail to our campsite. I stay behind with Sarah to make sure nobody has left anything on the beach. As we scan the brown sands and grassy areas surrounding us, she smiles and says "Quinn, I see what an excellent young lady you are, and it makes me regret all the hell I gave my parents when I was your age."

"I just like to help," I respond, but the rest of my sentence is cut short by the startling look in Sarah's eyes. Her gaze is fixed over my left shoulder, squinting to see something better. She walks slowly past me and over to a small clearing about twenty feet from where we all had set our beach towels. I follow her and see what appears to be a pile of garbage. As we get closer, I realize that it is a heap of smashed, empty beer cans and cigarettes put out in the sand. One of the beer cans on its side still has liquid pooled around it, telling me this mess couldn't have been made that long ago. Sarah simply stares at the scene for a few moments, and I can see the concern in her eyes.

"Hey, Quinn, will you grab one of the trash bags from my backpack and bring it down to me?"

"Of course," I say, slowly turning to grab my belongings and head to the site.

"Oh, and let's just keep this between us for now. I don't want any of the girls to be alarmed for no reason, you know what drama queens they can be."

"Roger that," I reply with a smile.

The girls are all so preoccupied with detangling their hair and unpacking the crates for dinner, nobody seems to have noticed that Sarah and I have been gone for the last ten minutes. When Jessie exits our tent, I simply act as if I was standing out here to give her privacy to get changed out of her swimsuit. She is none the wiser.

Although Sarah is doing her best to act like it's business as usual, I can see the worry in her eyes as she is giving us assignments for dinner. Surely if she thought there were a group of people near our campsite, she would have us move. She must assume that they've moved on and I'm sure they have, too.

She gives us each a role: some are to chop and prep the hobo dinners, some are to actually cook them and the rest of us will clean up the mess and walk down to the lake to hand wash the pots and pans used. Between chopping the potatoes, carrots and onions, seasoning the meat, and the trial and error of cooking over an open flame, it is nearly two hours before we finally eat. We are all starving and cranky. Sarah walks around the circle of girls sitting by the fire and pours us each a cup of milk from the gallon she's carrying.

"Don't you think it's a little offensive that we call these things hobo dinners? Why don't we just refer to them as tinfoil dinners?" Caroline leans over and asks me, apparently a little too loud because Cassie chuckles arrogantly.

"Does it occur to you that maybe the name is a tribute to hobos because they came up with the recipe?" she asks, with more than a hint of condescendence in her tone.

"Wait, I don't even know what a hobo is," I foolishly admit. This gets a roar of laughter from Cassie and her clique.

"You are *so* small town," Rachel quips.

"I mean, aren't we all?" I retort.

Sarah takes mercy on me and patiently explains that a hobo is a dated term for a homeless person and that, come to think of it, Caroline is absolutely right – maybe we should just call them tinfoil dinners going forward.

My job is to collect all the metal camping plates from the girls and bring them down to the lake to wash clean enough to pack for the journey home tomorrow. Jessie is assigned to the pots and pans and Samantha, Caroline's tent-mate, to the utensils. I grab an empty crate, a bottle of Dawn, and start walking around the circle to gather everyone's plates. When I get to Cassie's group, her friend Trishelle stares me straight in the eye and squirts off-brand ketchup all over her empty plate before handing it to me. This gets giggles from her dipshit friends. I wish I had the nerve to just slap her in the face with the gooey, red plate, but, alas, I'm still mildly terrified of these girls. I instead pretend not to notice and just stack it in the crate with the rest of them. Jessie and Samantha are standing by the entrance to the waterfront trail, dirty pans and utensils in their hands, waiting for me. I can see the pain in their eyes as they watch Trishelle's little prank go down. I shake it off and smile as I walk towards them with my full crate.

"This is my third year at Shady Oaks, and I have never seen anyone handle Cassie Huntington and her clique as well as you do, Quinn," Jessie speaks quietly as we make our way down to the lake.

"I will not give them the satisfaction of seeing me upset," I respond. "My mom taught me that."

"What happened to your mom?" Samantha asks, and I can see in her eyes that she instantly regrets how casually she asked the question.

"There's not much of a story. She just left. Now it's just me, my dad, and my stupid brother."

"I hate brothers," Samantha replies.

"Me too," adds Jessie.

This seems to satisfy her enough to change the subject. We discuss the boys in Aiden's cabin, A-2, for twenty minutes while we crouch over and wash dishes so long my back gets stiff, and my legs are numb.

By the time we get back up to the campsite, the fire is roaring, and Sarah is unloading supplies for s'mores. She tells us all to search for a stick that will be good for roasting marshmallows, and most of us find one within minutes. Mine is a little too fat on the end so Sarah reaches in her cargo shorts for her pocketknife and hands it to me to whittle down the end. In one year, I've gone from my mother making my bed and cutting my sandwiches for me, to being alone at camp for weeks and sharpening my own s'mores stick. I'm basically an adult.

As we each toast our marshmallows (Jessie likes golden brown, but I want mine on fire and crispy), Sarah asks if we want to hear any ghost stories. We are teenage girls on a camping trip, of course we want to hear ghost stories.

She animatedly tells us the legend of Timothy, one hand holding her s'more and the other wildly gesturing as she gives us all the haunting details.

She tells us that shortly after the camp opened in 1958, two campers named Timothy and Susan had a summer romance. They decided to sneak off and go swimming in the lake, which was then referred to as Lake 124, on a stormy August night. An hour into their little adventure, something began to pull Timothy under water. Susan tried to help him, but the force was too strong. He was pulled under and never seen again. Susan's screams could be heard throughout the camp. Timothy now haunts the camp, trying to find his lost love. Legend has it that he will do this until their souls reunite, but Susan is still alive somewhere in rural Wisconsin. His spirit tends to stick to the abandoned area of camp, as that is where their cabins were on the night Timothy died.

I might believe Sarah if she wasn't trying so hard to make us buy it. It had to be a lie; the truth was never that hard to sell.

My skepticism is interrupted by a deep, garish howl coming from the woods behind my back. The group is suddenly silent; we all heard it.

"What the hell kind of animal was that?" asks Cassie.

"Language," Sarah absentmindedly mumbles as she raises her finger to her lips to silence us.

The howl comes again, this time closer.

"Is it the dogman?" loudly whispers Rachel.

"The dogman isn't real, idiot," Cassie responds.

"But, what about what you said in the van?" Rachel asks.

"I was just trying to scare these morons," Cassie says as she vaguely gestures towards the log that Jessie, Caroline, and I are sitting on.

"It's probably just a wolf or a coyote," Sarah explains but her words are cut off by a third howl, this one morphing into the unmistakable sound of a man screaming.

Ten

Now

It's the Thursday before Memorial Day Weekend. Tomorrow, the survivors will descend upon Shady Oaks. The staff, the counselors, the campers; everyone who made it out alive and still possesses the desire to step foot on those grounds again. Those of us who walked out of the gates that Saturday morning in 1999 spent the following days being interviewed by police, months being questioned by strangers and years thinking about what happened that fateful night. Everyone wanted answers and none of us were able to provide enough to satisfy them.

The sun has just set and I'm lying awake in bed, replaying every moment of that summer. From the minute I met Aiden my first summer at camp to the last moments we spent together, my heart grew a thousand times bigger. I may have been sixteen, but I loved Aiden more than most people love in a lifetime. I thought about him every hour of every day. He set the bar for what kind of love I should have in my life and that is probably why I never married. I dated a string of second-rate men, including an author with a household name, but every relationship just had something missing. Aiden ignited a spark that lit my entire body on fire. I understand that's a heavy feeling for a teenager, but I remember it like it was yesterday.

I wonder what he's doing this very moment. I wonder if he's wishing that I'll show up. I can only hope that my dad's harsh words when he called the house didn't deter him from attempting to reach out again. Jessie, my brother Matt and his wife, and my father are the only people in my life who know I'm here. I'm not ready for anyone else to know yet.

If I were writing a character in my situation, I'd make her do something crazy. I'd write a scene where she gets out of this bed, throws her clothes on and heads straight for Shady Oaks to reunite with her long-lost love. I'd make the reunion pure magic. Readers would hang on every word through tear-soaked lashes. If it gets made into a movie, the scene would put Ryan Gosling and Rachel McAdams to shame. Who needs *The Notebook* when you have Shady Oaks?

After twenty minutes of laying out the entire scene – yes, the scene I would write in a fictitious account of my own situation – I hop out of bed. I'm not sure what has gotten into me. I just want to see the place before everyone gets there, so I can make my decision. I slip on my Keds and throw a Mackinac Island hoodie over my tank top and grey sweatpants. I peek in the mirror, although I don't know why; I'm not going to see anyone. I'm just going to walk to the edge of the grounds and see what he's done with the place. That's it. Easy peasy. No harm, no foul.

I take a half of a Xanax, just in case.

I take the other half for good measure.

I laugh because I remember how cool I thought it was when Sarah took prescription meds. Now I need them just to go outside.

I tiptoe down the stairs and leave Christy a note on the kitchen island, before grabbing a flashlight out of the drawer.

Christy,
I had to see it for myself.
I'll be careful and I'll be back.
If I don't come back, keep collecting that paycheck until someone notices I'm gone.
Xoxo
Q
PS Don't tell dad

Before I can think long enough to stop myself, I'm out the back door. I'm walking through the lush lawn; I'm hitting the edge of the trail on the back of my property. Flashes of Aiden are rapidly playing through my mind as I run down the trail, my flashlight illuminating the path before me.

Abercrombie cologne.

Tommy Bahama shorts.

The way he runs his hands through his hair every time I give him a compliment.

The way his dimples appear out of nowhere when he tells a joke.

The way he understood me like nobody ever had.

The Xanax is kicking in and I feel like I'm floating. I'm running through these woods, but I'm not the one controlling my motions. I'm on autopilot. My destination is Shady Oaks, and nothing is going to stop me.

Twenty minutes into my run, the trail empties out onto a gravel road. Yes, my home is in the middle of the same forest as Shady Oaks – but also, the same county. The same zip code. Brigadoon was built on a five-acre plot, just across the same small lake as the camp that changed my life. Lake Timothy. Maybe that's one of the many reasons I haven't disclosed my location to many people. I don't want to have to explain myself.

Two minutes down the gravel road and I look up to see the brand new, illuminated Shady Oaks sign. It's beautiful. Maybe dad will speak a little kinder of Aiden when he finds out he's the one who finally replaced the old sign.

I stay on the side of the drive and slowly walk towards the entrance of the camp, turning my flashlight off in the process. As I near the grounds, I can hear the late-night sounds of a staff preparing the camp for everyone's arrival. There are pots and pans clanging in the mess hall. Someone has a radio playing easy '70s hits. The full camp comes into view after the last turn, and it takes my breath away. It's exactly as it was; only better. The buildings have fresh stain on the wood. The totem pole has been restored. The canteen is lit and fully stocked. The grass is green and fresh. The entire area is lit by high-powered overhead lights, in addition to high wattage string lights hung throughout the camp. I can't believe he did it. He made the saddest place I know look like Disneyworld. Too bad I won't be here tomorrow to let him know.

I decide not to go any further, I don't want to risk being caught. I saw what I came to see: the transformation. I have hope that a new generation of kids will arrive this summer at Shady Oaks and have the time of their lives. All the pain of this place can be filed away and replaced with happy memories.

I turn to leave and choke back a scream as I realize there is a large man directly behind me. My hands rise to my face and then I stumble backwards, too stunned to run. I look at his face and a smile slowly spreads, his teeth a dazzling white.

It can't be.

"Aiden?"

Eleven

Then

The girls of cabin B-2 become celebrities overnight. Everyone wants to hear about our run-in with the dogman. Our brush with death. The most harrowing night of our lives.

The story, in reality, is a little anticlimactic. Sarah used her radio to contact camp, we hurriedly packed our bags and ran down the two-mile trail to the main road where a van driven by Dave (Hairy Legs) was waiting for us. The drive back to camp was spent in silence, mostly because we were all too stunned to speak, but also because we wanted to hear what Sarah and Dave were speaking about in hushed tones.

It is nearly midnight by the time we arrive back at Shady Oaks and sleepily make our way to the cabin while Dave volunteers to unpack the crates so Sarah can accompany us. None of us take the time to wash our faces or put our retainers in, we all simply collapse in our beds. I spend the next hour or two lying on my back, staring at the metal bed frame above me, and overanalyzing every noise I hear from outside the cabin. I know I'm not alone because normally I can hear the snores of at least a few girls if I wake in the middle of the night. Tonight, it's silent. Everyone must be too scared to sleep.

Morning reveille comes out of nowhere. I had just dozed off for what felt like thirty minutes when the trumpet sounds so loud, I swear he's playing right outside of our cabin door. I would rather do anything than get out of bed at this minute.

"Girls let's get up and grab some breakfast. I know everybody is tired, but the good news is that we were supposed to be hiking to the van after breakfast today, so our schedule is completely clear. We can come back here and rest for a few hours, I promise."

Sarah looks rough. We all do. I've never seen so many teenagers with bags under their eyes. Everyone is thinking about what happened last night, but nobody is talking.

It takes approximately ten minutes in the mess hall before word starts spreading. Of course, people wonder why the overnight cabin is at breakfast, when we should be at Shadow Lake. A few of the girls in our cabin give the cliff notes version of what happened, and it takes off. By the time we are done singing our morning songs, the other campers are fighting over who gets to talk to us as we leave the mess hall. The camp is in a frenzy. I just want to go back to the cabin, curl up in my sleeping bag and rest until I can think straight.

I'm a few feet out of the mess hall, walking with my head down, when a hand grabs me by my right arm.

I'm so jumpy, my first reaction is to flinch and shake it off.

"I'm so sorry, I was saying your name and you didn't seem to hear me. Are you good?"

There's something about Aiden's face that puts me at ease. I can't seem to put it into words. He just calms me. I've obviously never laid down with a boy, but I'd give anything for him to be able to come back to my bunk and just wrap his arms around me. I bet I'd sleep all day.

"Hey Aiden, sorry. I guess I'm in my own world."

"Is there anything I can do?" he asks.

"Honestly, I think I just need some sleep. I promise, I'll feel up to talking about it later. I'll tell you everything."

"Quinn, I don't need to hear any details, that's not why I caught up with you. I just wanted to make sure you're okay."

I stand there for a minute and look into his eyes. Normally my anxiety would prevent me from staring directly at him, but I'm too tired to care. He is beautiful. Even at fourteen, I've become pretty skilled at reading people and following my intuition. All I feel when I look in Aiden's eyes is safe.

"I appreciate that more than you know," I say with a slight smile. "I'm going to lie down for a couple hours. I'll see you at lunch?"

"It's a date," he says with a quick wink.

My plan is to lie in my bunk and visualize what a long-distance relationship with Aiden would be like. Neither of us have our driver's licenses; how would we ever see each other? I decide to make a mental list of how we will make it work, but I am out cold as soon as my head hits the pillow. Sarah has a cassette tape filled with the sounds of rain and thunderstorms; she plays it when she can't sleep. Today, she has placed her tape player in the middle of the cabin, has rewound the rain sounds to the beginning, and it's all any of us need to fall into a deep slumber.

I wake up and look at the alarm clock across the room by Sarah's bed; it's shortly after one in the afternoon. We've missed lunch. I sleepily look around the room – everyone is still passed out, except Caroline who is sitting up in bed and quietly reading a dogeared copy of the latest Goosebumps. I feel like I have slept for a year. My urge to pee is nearly unbearable so I grab my flip-flops and decide I'll put them on outside, as to not wake anyone. As soon as I'm upright, I realize Sarah isn't in her bed.

We've all learned the trick to alleviating the squeaking noise from the screen door: slowly open it a few inches and then quickly open it all the way. It's nearly silent. I smile to myself because after a week, I've aced the process. As I step onto the concrete landing outside the cabin, I hear voices speaking in hushed tones around the corner. I can't help myself; I stop and listen.

"I don't know, Pat. I mean, obviously it wasn't the dogman. It was just some creep trying to scare the girls."

"I don't like the thought of you alone in those woods with some man or men out there. I think we should start planning our overnights together."

"Oh, two cabins full of horny teenagers, allowed to camp together overnight? Dave will never allow it."

I grab onto the branch of an oak tree by the landing to steady myself so I can place my flip-flops on. I misjudge the distance and stumble off the three-inch concrete platform, shaking the tree in the process.

"Quinn?" Sarah asks as she rounds the corner.

"Sorry, I just woke up and I have to pee so bad," I say, feeling my face turn slightly red.

She doesn't seem angry at all that I was eavesdropping. Or maybe she doesn't realize.

"I let you girls sleep through lunch, I figured you needed it. Marge is packing up a basket full of sandwiches and chips for you, I'm just on my way to go grab them. How about I follow you to the latrine and then we'll swing by the kitchen, and you can help me carry them back?"

"Deal," I smile.

"Is Pat your boyfriend?" I ask as I'm drying my hands. Sarah is leaned up against the wall, waiting for me.

"Well, I suppose he is. But that's top secret. We aren't supposed to have relationships with fellow staff, so I'm trusting you, Harstead," she answers.

"He stares at you all day, I don't think it's a very well-kept secret," I respond, and she laughs.

"You might be right."

Each girl wakes from her much-needed slumber and we all sit up in our beds and eat the lunches that Marge has prepared for us with the kind of euphoria that can only come from a hard afternoon nap. We are all crunching on our Old Dutch chips when Sarah announces that she'd like to talk to us about what happened last night.

"You girls aren't children. There's no need to shield you from things like I would with the nine and ten-year-old cabin. We believe that there was a man or men that had been partying in the woods before we arrived at Shadow Lake. He or they probably saw a cabin full of teenagers and thought it would be fun to scare us."

Nobody responds. We all consider the possibility of this theory, until Rachel speaks up.

"Why won't you admit it could have been the dogman?"

Sarah smiles sympathetically.

"Guys, the dogman is an urban legend. It was made up to spook people, just like the legend of Timothy."

"So, you're telling us that is made up, too?" asks Caroline.

"Look, I wasn't around in 1958, so I can't tell you for sure, but I believe the counselors just made it up for a good campfire story. I've been here for five summers, and I swear, the story changes a little each year," Sarah says.

"The good news is," she continues, "what happened to us last night is going to be camp lore for decades to come. The night that the B-2 girls basically came face-to-face with the dogman. You ladies are going to be legends."

Twelve

It's Friday night, the final night of camp for the summer of 1997. The last few days have been spent trying to forget about the terror of our overnight, fielding questions from nosy campers, and trying my best to cross paths with Aiden as much as possible.

On Tuesday, he took my tray from me at lunch and emptied it in the garbage. Before I could thank him, Pat stepped between us and asked for Aiden's help loading up canoes for an afternoon river trip.

On Wednesday, Jessie and I went to the arts and crafts building to check on our dreamcatchers and ran into Aiden and Vinny sword fighting with their freshly painted walking sticks just outside the building. Our conversation was interrupted by the art teacher scolding the boys for acting like clowns.

On Thursday, Jake asked Jessie for her address so they could keep in touch through the winter. I had never been so jealous in my life. Aiden and Vinny witnessed the transaction as Jake and Jessie nervously wrote down their contact information and then high-fived their friend for his victory.

Now, we are all getting ready for the final night dance. Dave told us all at lunch that we would learn traditional moves from Russia, South America, Germany, and more. Learning these dances will be a skill that we will "take with us wherever we go in life."

I can assure you, none of us give a damn about learning new dance moves. We all just want to look good enough to catch the attention of whichever boy we've become smitten with over the last two weeks and have enough rhythm to not make complete fools of ourselves.

Cassie is hogging the full-length mirror in the corner of the cabin, so the rest of us are getting ready using the small mirrors that come in our dusty Cover Girl compacts. There are curling irons plugged into every outlet in the cabin and the overwhelming smell of charred hair and Aqua Net is nearly too much to handle.

I catch a break when Cassie momentarily walks away from obsessing over herself, and I quickly scramble over to the mirror. Jessie did my hair and makeup, which consists of spiral curls held by bobby pins on top of my head and some pink lip gloss with blush to match. I'm wearing a navy-blue dress with yellow sunflowers that falls just above my knees. My black slip-on wedges complete the look, although I forgot to bring nail polish so my naked toenails peeking out at the edge are a bit of an eyesore.

It's not very often at all that I have felt pretty in my life, but tonight I do. I'm just tan enough to cover my hiking-related bruises and the bumps from old mosquito bites. If I were an outsider looking in, I might even say "This girl looks good enough to be in the pages of a Delia's catalog."

Although I'm not as skilled as Jessie, I helped as much as I could with her hair and makeup, and she looks great. Her sandy blond hair was a little too thin to hold curls, but I did tease it a bit and inserted a few rhinestone-encrusted barrettes on each side. I let her borrow my other dress, the one I brought as a backup. It's pale yellow with white daisies printed on the straps and looks perfect with her golden-brown skin. I wave her over to stand in the mirror next to me. I can tell by the look in her eyes that she's never seen herself like this. I wonder if her and her friends back home ever do each other's makeup. She hasn't said much at all about her friends in Iron River.

"You look like a supermodel," I tell her.

"*We* look like supermodels," she corrects me.

I aim my camera towards the mirror and take a picture of us in the reflection. Maybe I'll frame it for my room when I get back home.

The ten of us girls walk to the dance together, each of us careful to avoid mud puddles from the brief afternoon rain we had a few hours earlier. The doors to the mess hall are propped open, and I can see that white Christmas lights have been strung throughout the venue. All the tables we normally sit at for meals have been pushed to one side of the hall and the other side is completely open. The wooden floors have been swept and mopped, and there is a punch bowl in the corner with a stack of empty cups next to it. It really looks like every middle school dance I've attended, only with a touch more magic.

All the counselors are dressed up; even Sarah's stupid boyfriend Pat looks handsome as he enters the hall in his Polo shirt and khaki pants. My heart beats a little faster when I see him, because I know Aiden will be closely behind. Vinny and Jake lead the rest of the cabin through the double doors. They both look nice with their slicked back hair and button-down shirts. I don't see Aiden and I worry that he may not be feeling well. I will be devastated if I don't get to dance with him tonight.

Everyone is standing around, awkwardly mingling, when I see Aiden hurriedly walk through the doors. He smiles when he sees me and makes a beeline in my direction. I think I might pass out. When he reaches me, he pulls a single sunflower out from behind his back, shows it to me, and reaches forward to stick it into the curls that are pinned to the top of my head.

"I saw you through the window when we were walking up. As soon as I saw the sunflowers on your dress, I remembered a patch of them I walked by earlier next to the totem pole, so I ran to pick one. It looks perfect. You look perfect."

I didn't really have a favorite flower until this very moment.

"That is the most thoughtful thing anyone has ever done for me," I respond.

"If that's the truth, you've got a really sad life and need some better friends," he laughs.

I smile and we are interrupted by Dave, whose hairy legs are covered by light grey dress pants, holding a megaphone, and announcing that the dance is about to begin.

I quickly learn that this "dance" isn't going to be like the ones at school, where we move awkwardly and slowly to Boyz II Men and pray the lights never come on again. No, much like every time that music has been played in this mess hall since our arrival, this is ridiculous. The songs are entirely too fast, the instructions are unclear, partners are switched every time we turn around and I can barely catch my breath. Against all odds...it is amazing. A complete blast. I don't think I've laughed this hard since before mom left.

Despite doing this several times a summer, hardly any of the staff can keep up. Marge is line dancing with both janitors. Dave dips the arts and crafts teacher so low her head almost hits the ground. Aiden keeps sneaking over to cheat the rules and be my partner again. Vinny is flirting with every girl in a three-cabin radius. Even Caroline is laughing. This night is magic.

Before we know it, Dave is thanking the dance instructors, the counselors, and the staff for a fun night. He says we all have an hour to get ready for bed before taps is played. We all leave the hall but linger in the front of it for a while to talk, since we have a rare full hour of freedom. We are teasing Vinny about his two left feet when Aiden leans over to tell me that my sunflower is gone.

"Oh, no," I say as I reach my hand up to confirm it.

"Let's go get you another one," he suggests with a smile. He senses my hesitancy and knows by now that I'm a rule-follower. "Quinn, there are no laws against us walking over to the totem pole, I promise you."

I smile and nod. The conversation continues as we sneak away; I think everyone is too drunk on joy to notice.

Just as he said, there's a bountiful patch of towering sunflowers right next to the pole. He bends to pick one up, snaps off the bulk of the stem, and sticks it into my hair, just where he placed the last one.

"Be more careful with this one," he says.

Before I can respond, he does the unthinkable.

He kisses me.

Its quick, it's innocent, but it's everything I've ever wanted. I'm floating.

"Maybe at breakfast tomorrow, we can exchange information and try to keep in touch this year?" he asks.

"I thought you'd never ask."

Thirteen

Now

"Quinn," he responds. Neither of us is moving. I have been thinking of this man every day for the last twenty-three years and now he is standing in front of me. I know he's thought of me, too. A love like we had doesn't just disappear.

"I didn't think you'd come. I tried to call your house, it's the only number I had for you. Your dad screamed at me and hung up before I could tell him why I was calling."

I smile.

"Now, that doesn't sound like the Jim Harstead I know. Maybe you had the wrong number."

He smiles, too.

"I've missed you, Quinn."

"I shouldn't even be here. But someday, somewhere else, we have a lot to talk about."

He raises his hands and lightly grabs both of my elbows, staring into my eyes. My knees nearly buckle. The last time I saw a picture of him was when he was on the cover of a tech magazine in my doctor's waiting room about six or seven years ago. The picture didn't do him justice. His face has filled out and his hair is cut a lot shorter, but his chocolate eyes are the same. I can't help but glance down at his left hand gripped around my arm, pulling me closer. There's no ring.

"I know we have a lot to talk about, but tonight I just want to tell you I miss you and how I've spent every single day hoping that you'd come."

He breaks my gaze for a moment and looks around us.

"Where did you park? Did you hide your car?"

I don't even want to begin the conversation of how I live within walking distance of the camp that nearly ruined our lives.

"It's a long story."

He directs me to an illuminated bench next to the totem pole and I notice that there are fresh sunflowers planted all around us as we sit. I touch the end of one and look to Aiden as he smiles just enough for his dimples to show.

"Nice touch," I tell him.

We sit and talk for nearly an hour. He tells me that he's been living near Detroit but dreaming of coming home for years. An investment banker called him when the Shady Oaks property went to auction, and Aiden ended up being the only bidder. Nobody else would touch a property with its history. He contacted a lot of the old staff and, surprisingly, most of them were on board with being involved in the reopening.

Although most of the campers have their own busy lives and won't be able to make it this weekend, he did have thirty RSVP yes, in addition to ten of the staff members. He can barely contain his excitement over the weekend's festivities and the plan to share his dreams for Shady Oaks with everyone. He even started a non-profit to raise funds for the kids whose families can't afford to send them.

"Dave has offered to reclaim his title as Camp Director," he tells me.

"Dave is still alive?" I gasp.

"Quinn, he was like thirty-five that summer. Yes, he's still alive," he laughs.

"How in the hell did these adults seem so old?"

"Dave will be back, and several of the children of the counselors have signed up to work for the summer. We have a full roster of kids for five two-week sessions, starting the first week of June."

"I can't believe you're doing this, Aiden. I just can't believe it. You're a stronger person than I am."

Aiden places his hand over mine, which is resting on my knee. He intertwines our fingers and my heart leaps.

"This place held a lot of special memories for a lot of people before it came crashing down. I think we can start over and show a new generation how wonderful Shady Oaks can be. I'd love for you to be involved. We have a bond forever, because of what we've been through together. Will you at least stay for the weekend? Please?"

There are a million reasons why I can't stay for the weekend. Why I shouldn't stay for the weekend. Countless reasons why it is a horrible idea.

"Aren't I public enemy number one?" I ask.

"Everyone I've talked to has been excited about the possibility of you showing up. I promise."

I take a moment to consider my options and, once again, think about how I'd write the scene for a character in my situation.

"Well, I better go home and pack," I smile.

Fourteen

Then

The month that I arrive home from camp is pure bliss. I'm on cloud nine. I tell every one of my neighborhood friends to keep the secret of my long-distance boyfriend, knowing full well that they will tell everyone they encounter. I'm in love and I want to shout it from the rooftops. I'm in such a good mood, I fill in mom's role at home and take on all the cooking and cleaning. Dad is thrilled. My life has meaning again.

Each day I run down our driveway when I hear the mail truck approaching and anxiously flip through the bills to see if there is a letter from Aiden. I constantly lift the receiver to the phone in our kitchen to make sure it's working. I pace back and forth in front of dad when he's talking to his buddies to make sure there's not a call waiting alert that he's ignoring. I dig out my mom's old cassette tapes and play "Please Mr.

Postman" on repeat. I'm singing *there must be some word today, from my boyfriend so far away* as I gaze out the window on a rainy day and finally, dad puts two-and-two together.

"Oh, Christ, don't tell me you met some slick little boy at that damn camp," he says as he stares at me sitting in the seat of the picture window with a hand full of Kleenex.

"I'm just having a bad day!" I yell, before running to my room and slamming the door.

"Thank God this is the last teenager I will ever raise," I hear him mumble.

For days I lie in my bed and wait to hear from him. I understand what true heartache feels like, at fourteen-years-old no less. I wonder if anyone hurts the way I do. I should be heading to the mall with my friends and buying clothes for my high school debut next week. My very first day of freshman year is approaching and I don't have a clue what I will wear, nor do I care in this moment.

One sunny Tuesday afternoon, I'm home alone while dad works a construction job in Escanaba when the phone rings. I gasp when I see the display on the caller ID: BROOKS, GLENN

I let it ring twice – you know, *play it cool.*

"Harstead residence," I answer nonchalantly.

"Is this Quinn?"

"Sorry, who is this?" I deserve an award for this performance.

"Quinn, it's Aiden. From camp."

Play it cool. Play it cool.

"Oh, Aiden, now I remember! How are you?"

Awkward silence.

102

"Did you just pretend that you had to take a minute to remember who I am?"

"I...just didn't hear who you said at first. I thought you said Kaden. Must be a bad connection."

More awkward silence.

"Sorry it took me so long to call, we've been down in Florida packing up our house and getting everything moved to Menominee. I left the paper with your information in Michigan, so I've been dying to contact you this whole time with no way to do it."

I finally unclench my jaw and drop my shoulders. I exhale. Of course, this is why it has taken him so long!

"I suppose it has been a while, not that I noticed."

He lets out a short "hah" and I can feel him smiling. It's radiating through the phone.

"So, how's life in Gladstone?" he asks.

We spend the next thirty minutes talking about school, sports, camp friends, and the new puppy his parents bought for his little sister. He promises to write me a letter once school starts so we can keep in touch without worrying about the nightmare of either of our parents answering when we call.

I cannot believe I just wasted over a month of my life completely wrecked with heartache when there wasn't even a reason to be sad. He's just a typical fourteen-year-old boy and he forgot my number back home in Michigan.

My life goes back to normal, or as normal as it can get starting high school without mom around, and I still wait by the phone and the mailbox, but not nearly as desperate. I have my few close friends, trombone lessons, and creative writing to keep me busy. My teacher, Miss Davis, says that I have a knack for writing and may even be able to do it for a living one day.

The weeks turn into months, and we are soon in the dead of winter in northern Michigan, which is not for the weak of heart. This town holds onto its winters like its people, with an iron grip that never lets go. I feel like I haven't seen the sun in months and if I don't hear from Aiden soon, I'm going to lose it. I wonder every day what a boy from Florida is doing during his first real Michigan winter. I want to ask him all about it. I hope his family isn't regretting their decision to move north.

Two days before Christmas, I receive a card from him. The front has two snowmen holding hands and the inside is blank, except for his handwriting. *Thinking of you, hope your Christmas is great. Which weeks will you be going to camp this summer? Love, Aiden*

This gives me the jolt of optimism I needed. Summer is on the horizon. We are talking about camp already. Camp, glorious Camp Shady Oaks, where I will spend two magical weeks with Aiden. There is no possibility of dad ever agreeing to drive me to Menominee, and my brother Matt moved up north for his railroad job. I know that camp is my only hope of seeing Aiden until we are old enough to drive. I just need to have the patience to wait for seven more months. I can do this.

Fifteen

Now

I float back home through the dark woods and narrow trail to Brigadoon, admiring the stars and appreciating the sounds. There's no rush, the anticipation is over. I'm not sure I've ever felt such relief. I saw Aiden and he doesn't hate me. I saw Shady Oaks and I didn't have a mental breakdown. I may be a little stronger than I give myself credit for.

As I near the back of the house, I can see through the window that there's a lamp turned on in the study, next to the kitchen. I try to remember if it was on when I left, but I was in such a hurry I don't recall much of anything.

I slowly slide the back patio door open and tiptoe inside. I turn to enter my code, so the alarm won't sound, when her voice nearly makes me jump out of my skin.

"You might have gotten away with it, had you remembered to disarm that alarm when you left," Christy says, sitting comfortably in the reading chair in the study. She's wearing a blue nightgown and drinking a mug of hot tea. I glance at the clock and see its just after midnight.

"I'm so sorry Christy...I left you a note."

"Quinn, when I took this job, I promised your dad that I would look after your wellbeing at all times. Do you care to guess what he would say to me if he knew you wandered out the door in the middle of the night?"

My instant reaction is to act defensively and explain to her that I'm an adult and it's technically not the middle of the night, but my therapist and I have been working on this. I take a deep breath and put myself in Christy's shoes. This is her livelihood. I would have been furious.

"I'm sorry, Christy. It won't happen again."

She reaches forward and pats the seat of the empty reading chair opposite hers.

"Well, you might as well come and tell me about it," she rolls her eyes with a reluctant smile.

I tell her everything. How beautiful the renovations are. How great it felt to hear sounds of life coming from the mess hall again. How great it felt to run through the woods. How great it felt to see Aiden.

"Did you ask him any of the questions you wrote down in therapy?" Christy asks, the concern in her eyes reminding me of my mother.

"He told me we could talk about everything this weekend. I was so overwhelmed with seeing him, it's like every question I had regarding his behavior was lost."

"This weekend? Does that mean you're going to go?" Christy asks.

"I think I am, Christy. I'll be gone until Monday, so go enjoy the holiday weekend. Do something fun."

She leans back in her chair, takes a sip of tea, and considers the possibility.

"I suppose I could go see my mother in Manistique. She's been nagging me about a visit. Just promise me you'll be careful."

I put my hand over hers and squeeze.

"I appreciate all you do for me, more than you know."

The lines around her eyes confirm the weight of everything she's done for me over the years.

"I know you do, Quinn. I know you do."

We sit in silence for a few moments, both of us contemplating what this weekend means. It will be my first night spent outside of Brigadoon in years. I'm not entirely sure where my suitcases are even kept. This will be yet another process that requires Christy's assistance.

"They say you never lose sight of your first love. That love never really leaves you, no matter how many years pass. I'm so happy that you and Aiden may have a second chance, but please remember that those grounds hold a different meaning for a lot of folks. Some people will never get their happy ending."

Sixteen

Then

There's something strange about seeing people only in the summer. There is no gradual change or growth to witness; it's abrupt.

"Quinn!" shouts a familiar voice as I'm grabbing my suitcase out of the back of dad's truck. It's Jessie, but I swear she has grown three inches. Her dirty blond hair is cut to her shoulders, and she has braces. I sprint to hug her, and she lifts me off the ground with ease. Once we are facing each other, I strain my neck to look her in the eyes.

"Did you go through a body stretcher? What the hell, Jess?"

She throws her head back and laughs.

"Not all of us are destined to be 5'2" for life, Quinn."

I punch her arm. It's like no time has passed at all.

"You must be Mr. Harstead. I'm Jessie Broeders, Quinn's friend from last summer," she says and extends a bony hand in dad's direction.

"Well, hello, Jessie. It's nice to finally meet you. Are your parents around? I'd be happy to meet them, so they feel comfortable letting you spend time with Quinnie this fall," he responds while looking around to spot them. "You're welcome at our home in Gladstone any time."

"Oh, they aren't here," she responds, a slight color rising in her cheeks. "But I would love to come visit Quinn this year, if you'll have me."

Dad realizes the situation and adapts quickly. He has conducted himself with a lot more dignity after a full year of being a single parent. Normally, mom would be good cop to his inappropriate cop.

"It would be our pleasure."

Jessie walks me to my cabin after we grab my second suitcase out of dad's truck, and I insist that I don't need him to help me unpack this year. He agreed, but his tight smile told me that he was a little emotional over his youngest daughter's newfound independence.

"Wow, B-1, the *adult's* cabin," Jessie marvels as we step inside.

"You'll be here with me next year, Jess," I remind her. "It's just one summer apart."

She nods, hands in her pockets as she looks around in amazement at what is the exact replica of the other B cabins. There is no difference, other than the lack of a squeaking in the screen door springs.

"Two weeks without Cassie Huntington? I think I'll be just fine."

I smile and throw my suitcase on a single bed, next to the window. No need to suffer through sleeping on the bottom bunk for the sake of making a friend this year.

"Maybe she won't even show up this year," I suggest but we both laugh before I even get the words out. Of course, she's showing up.

Jessie helps me stretch my sheets out over the mattress and hang my clothes in the cubby, despite my insistence that I don't need her help. I think she just wants to hang around to see who else shows up for cabin B-1.

Within fifteen minutes, Cassie predictably makes her entrance, alongside Trishelle and Rachel. Heaven forbid they spend a moment apart. She makes one rude comment about Jessie not reaching the age requirement to be in our cabin and moves on. She has unfortunately grown more beautiful over the last twelve months. Two girls I remember from last year come together – Erin and Samantha. The last four girls arrive alone and are either new campers or they attended different sessions last year. Sure enough, as soon as the last girl arrives, Jessie bids me adieu and heads back to her own cabin.

Sarah comes strolling through the cabin door, as beautiful as ever. She's like the older sister I've always wanted. I don't realize how fond of her I am until I find myself tearing up over her arrival.

"Sarah!" gasps one of the girls I don't recognize.

"Hey ladies, I got transferred to the fifteen and sixteen-year-old cabins this summer! Can you believe it?"

We all gather around her to hear about the excitement of her off-season. She's getting her master's degree from Michigan State University and only has one year left, so next summer will be her last at Shady Oaks. That's okay because it will be my last as well.

"This is my first all-veteran cabin, ever. There isn't a single new camper. This means we are going to have a blast the next two weeks and I won't be stopping to give directions!" she shouts and claps her perfectly manicured hands in excitement.

We have an hour before "Welcome Dinner," so I head to my bed to grab my camera and go find Jessie. I feel the presence of someone behind me as I bend over to reach in my suitcase.

"So, how was your first year at Gladstone?"

I spin around quickly because the voice almost sounds like Cassie Huntington, but that miserable cow would never take the time to ask about someone else's life unless there was an ulterior motive.

Sure enough, it's her.

"Just fine, Cassie. How is Marquette?"

She rolls her eyes and then pulls the expensive sunglasses from the top of her head and cleans them on her Ralph Lauren tank top.

"It's Marquette. It's whatever. I can't wait to graduate so I can study abroad and get the hell out of Michigan."

What a Cassie answer that is.

"Anyway," she continues, "Did you hear from Aiden at all while you were home?"

My heart sinks.

"Yeah, a few times. Why?"

"Well, Vinny's insignificant ass promised to call me, and he never did. Not that I care. I just know that they do everything together, so I wasn't sure if you saw him this winter. Again, not that I care."

Oh.

"I mean, I didn't see Aiden at all. Also, I didn't know you and Vinny were…"

She quickly puts her sunglasses back on.

"We're not," she snaps. "I just think it's funny that he said he'd call and didn't. I guess I wanted to make sure he was still alive or whatever."

She doesn't give me time to respond before she walks across the cabin to grab her crew and hurries out the door.

I can't help but smile. Somebody has got Cassie Huntington flustered. I need to high-five Vinny when I see him, but first I need to check myself in the mirror before I head out of the cabin. I haven't talked to Aiden since Easter, but I mentioned meeting him in the spot where we first met, next to the volleyball courts. Hopefully he remembers.

I glance in the full-length mirror next to Sarah's bed.

Butterfly clips placed perfectly in my curls. Love Spell lotion rubbed on every inch of my limbs. The scent of Big Red gum radiating from my breath. Tommy Hilfiger jean shorts that I saved months for. Check, check, check.

I'm ready to go.

When I leave the cabin, Jessie is waiting outside for me.

"That bad?" I ask.

We begin walking in stride together towards the activity area, just picking up right where we left off.

"The only person I know is Caroline. The counselor is brand new and from Minnesota. There are two girls from a different session last year and all the rest are newbies. Are you kidding me, a cabin full of rookies?"

I playfully slap her arm.

"I was a newbie last year and you did just fine with me," I remind her.

"You weren't nearly as annoying as I expected you to be. It's going to take everything in me to make it through the next two weeks."

"I've got an idea," I propose. "Why don't we write letters to each other, kind of like writing letters home, but we don't give them to each other until the last day? That way we can go home and read all about what camp was like in the other cabin."

She's silent for a moment and runs her hand through her straight hair, placing it behind her ear.

"I love it," she smiles. "I think that's a great idea!"

Everything about this year already feels better than the last, even though she's in another cabin. I feel more confident, comfortable with my surroundings, and prepared for the next two weeks. I know what to expect and that puts me at ease.

As we near the activity area, I see Aiden and Vinny playing tetherball with Jake and another boy from their cabin last year. I walk a little slower and pull down on the hem of my shorts.

"Relax, you look great," Jessie smiles. I see her look at Jake and wave.

"Did you see him in the off-season?" I ask.

"Yeah, he goes to Crystal Falls and his big brother is a senior, so he drives. I think we spent almost every weekend together."

"I am so jealous." I can't imagine spending every weekend with Aiden. I'd die of happiness.

"Quinnie Q!" shouts Aiden with a casual tone, as if he saw me just last week. He overheard my dad call me that one time when he answered the phone and shouted for me, and I have yet to live it down. He thinks it's hilarious.

"I asked you not to call me that in public," I smile as he approaches me, arms out. We hug tightly and I realize it's our first real hug. Sure, we had that quick yet perfect kiss by the totem pole, but by the time breakfast was over the next morning, parents were beginning to show up and we were both too shy to touch each other at all while saying goodbye.

I spent the drive here today mentally preparing myself to be standoffish with Aiden because I was irritated with how little we communicated in the past year. Four phone calls and two letters; that's it. That is not nearly enough to pacify a love-drunk fourteen (now fifteen) year-old for an entire year. My friend Monica's older sister assured me that all boys our age are complete idiots, and he probably thinks he's doing his absolute best. Just because it's true doesn't mean I have to like it.

All my plans to punish Aiden with the silent treatment were thrown out the window the minute I saw him. I don't know how it's possible for a boy I've spent two weeks with to feel like home, but he does.

We pull away from each other (although I don't want to; he smells like sandalwood and minty gum), and Vinny walks up and gives me a quick side hug. I'm basically part of the family.

"Vinny Brooks, you're apparently in big trouble for not calling Cassie this winter," I tease.

Aiden laughs and grips both of Vinny's shoulders as he throws his head back in defeat.

"If you think I have time for the kind of chaos that Cassie Huntington brings, you are mistaken. I was a freshman starter for football *and* basketball this year. Coach said no distractions," he says.

"Oh, is that why I barely heard from your cousin? Was he a starter, too?" I laugh.

I can't believe the amount of confidence I've developed over the last year. Just one year ago, I was standing in this very spot, getting pegged in the forehead by a low-flying volleyball. Now I'm effortlessly cracking jokes with the best-looking boys at camp.

"Maybe you didn't hear from him because he was too busy talking about you every five minutes," Vinny laughs as Aiden rolls his eyes.

"Not true," Aiden smiles.

I scan the activity area and see Jessie sitting atop one of the picnic tables with Jake. They are sitting so closely; their knees are touching. She catches my gaze and smiles so big the sun reflects off her braces. I snap a quick picture with my disposable camera.

I briefly think about the few friends I have back home and feel guilty knowing that there's no way they are having this good of a summer. I wish everyone my age got to experience Shady Oaks at least once in their lives.

As we take our seats for welcome dinner, the confidence I feel radiates through my body. I know the staff, nearly all the counselors, and recognize most of the campers. I know the routine, I know what Dave will say next, I know we will be "haunted" by Timothy at the lake after dinner tonight. I suddenly understand why families tend to vacation in the same places year after year; it begins to feel like home.

The only difference in tonight's camp introduction is the mention of Shady Oaks 40th anniversary – fun by the lake since 1958! Forty years of memories in the Hiawatha National Forest! This calls for celebration. Our final weekend at camp will include appearances from a few campers who attended in that first season and, even more exciting, cake and ice cream to celebrate the milestone.

Later, as we take our seats on the wooden log benches at the lake front, it feels strange not to be sitting by Jessie. This is just one of those camp activities that require the cabins to sit together, so I'm stuck with my B-1 crew. Luckily, it appears Sarah and Pat must still be together because our cabin is seated in front of his. Also in our favor is the fact that Pat apparently got promoted to the fifteen and sixteen-year-old cabins this summer as well.

I spot Aiden, Vinny, and Jake and take a seat directly in front of them. Thankfully, Samantha and Erin from my cabin sit next to me so there's no room for Cassie. I don't need her dramatics scaring Vinny off tonight.

Dave begins his welcome night routine and, glancing around at the faces of the other campers, it's obvious who is attending camp for the first time. They all have the same look of wonder that I did last summer. From the corner of my eye, I see Pat crouch and leave his spot next to the boys to go hide in the woods and change into his "Timothy" costume. I turn my head and wink at Aiden, who is smiling back at me.

The sun is setting over the lake as Dave and the rest of the counselors build the giant fire in the same spot on the beach in front of us. I feel the comfort of watching an old movie I've seen before as they start chanting about Timothy around the crackling flames. I feel Aiden's hands reach up and gently start to play with my curls, which are flowing loose halfway down my back. He's methodically running his fingers through them, like it's second nature to him.

"Your hair smells so good. Like strawberries," he bends forward and whispers in my ear.

I take a deep breath. I've never been so relaxed.

Seventeen

My days at camp fall into a blissful routine. Breakfast. Swim Class. Free Time. Lunch. Arts and Crafts. Quiet Hour. Nature Hour. Dinner. Free Time. Write a letter to Jessie to tell her everything she wasn't around to see, tuck it in my backpack, get ready for bed. Rinse and repeat. Every minute of free time is spent at the activity courts with Jessie, Aiden, and the rest of the crew. Occasionally, Cassie and her friends come uninvited to sit with us, but I don't mind because Aiden doesn't pay them any attention.

I absolutely love that Vinny won't give her the time of day; it makes her seem a little more human to me. She basically throws herself at him whenever she and the clique are around, and he barely seems to notice. It's beautiful.

At lunch each day, Dave does mail call and shouts the names of campers who have received a letter or (better yet) a package from home. Last year, I got one letter from my Aunt Betty and nothing from dad.

118

Although my feelings were a little hurt, I understood. Jessie didn't get any packages either.

I normally tune out as he is doing mail call to distract myself from the jealousy I feel towards the campers who get boxes filled with chocolate, chips, and magazines from their loving parents. I know there must be a mistake when Dave yells, "Quinn Harstead," while holding a medium-sized brown package. He repeats himself, scanning the room for a camper to stand and approach him so he can set it on the table in front of him and move onto the next. Jessie nudges me hard. I walk slowly to the center of the mess hall, fully preparing myself for the embarrassment of walking back to my seat empty-handed after learning that he made a mistake.

When I'm within a few feet of the table, I recognize dad's sloppy handwriting on the box. I can't believe it. Dad sent me a package. I grab it very nonchalantly and tuck it under my left arm, as if I receive care packages all the time. I sit back down and casually set the box next to me while I finish my cherry pie, but I can feel Jessie staring at me.

"C'mon, Quinn, it's the first time either of us has gotten a package; you're really not going to open it?"

She's right. I don't need to be playing it cool. My dad, who doesn't have the patience required to use his blinker ("*It's nobody's damned business where I'm turning*") has sat down, filled a box, taped it shut, and drove it to the post office to send to me. This also required him to look up the mailing address for camp in the welcome packet we received, which makes this an even grander miracle.

"You're right." I smile and begin tearing open the tape. Several small items are separated by crumpled up pages from The Daily Press.

The package contains: one box of Girl Scout cookies (which he was no doubt conned into buying by little Nicole next door), one can of Pepsi with a dent in it, one bag of Skittles, a pack of gum with two pieces missing, a half-used bottle of sunscreen, and what appears to be a letter. I slowly unfold it to discover it is our water bill from two months ago, on the back of which he has written me a note in Sharpie.

Quinnie Q, I would have sent money, but I had already taped the box shut. Xoxo Dad

Always a comedian.

"You're so lucky," Jessie says, her lips barely curling into a slight smile. *I'm lucky.* I'm one of the lucky kids whose parent sent them a package. Although it was filled with completely random items and smelled faintly of cigarette smoke, I know dad did his best.

"Do you want to talk to me about your parents?" I ask with hesitance. This is my second summer with Jessie, and she has yet to mention them at all.

"When they decide to act like parents, they aren't so bad. When they are on benders and off with their friends, I'm left to fend for myself. The only reason I'm here is because one of my teachers helped me get a county-sponsored spot. I doubt my mom and dad even realize I'm gone."

My heart breaks in a thousand pieces. No matter how bad I tell myself I have it at home, my problems are nothing compared to hers. My dad might be a foul-mouthed contractor, but he's home every night to make sure I'm fed and in bed on time for school.

"Seeing normal families hurts, doesn't it?" she asks.

"Yeah. Yeah, it does."

"At least your dad is trying."

"You're right, I probably need to give him more credit."

Jessie nods and, for the first time, I understand why she has crow's feet at her age. I know why she shows up to camp alone. I know why she has so many survival skills and why she is so independent. That's when I make the promise, to myself, that I will always be there for her. Whatever she needs in life, I'll be right here to help.

After dinner that night, we get an unexpected thunderstorm. Dave said it was supposed to miss us entirely, but the storm changes paths and stays directly above Shady Oaks for an eternity. It pours buckets on our little cabin, and the girls and I roll up our beach towels and put them at the base of the screen door to stop the water from coming in. The thunder booms louder than anything I had ever heard, and the lightning lights up the sky every minute or so. Roughly an hour into the storm, a giant flash illuminates the woods around us, and the entire camp loses power. Luckily, flashlights are at the top of the required packing list that Shady Oaks sends our parents, so we are well equipped.

Sarah is calm, cool, and collected as she asks us each to join her on the floor in the center of the cabin. The ten of us form a circle, most of us with our sleeping bags wrapped snuggly around our shoulders. Sarah lights a chunky white candle in the middle of our circle and slowly backs away, sitting between Samantha and me.

"Raise your hand if you were in my cabin last year when we encountered the dogman," she says, shining her flashlight back and forth among us.

Cassie, Rachel, Trishelle, Erin, Samantha, and I all raise our hands. That leaves only four girls that weren't present for our night of terror.

"Well, I could probably be fired for telling you this, so I need everyone to raise their pinkies and put them in the center of the circle, over the flame. Everyone has to swear that this will never leave this room."

We all do as we are told.

She looks around the circle at our faces, the candle flame flickering in the whites of our eyes, before continuing.

"Obviously, we called the State Police to investigate the screams we heard. We told them all about the beer cans that were left behind when we arrived at the site," she says, her eyes focused on the ground. She seems to be wrestling with herself over whether to tell us any more of the story.

"About a month after the last camp session ended, Dave called me to come back to Shady Oaks for a meeting. When I walked in, the rest of the counselors were there, along with two police officers."

She pauses for entirely too long.

"Well, what did they say?" Cassie basically shouts.

"I'll leave out all the gory details, but basically they found the men that had been drinking at the campsite before we got there. They had been murdered, less than one hundred yards from our tents. There are

122

no suspects and Dave has been doing everything he can to keep it out of the papers."

We all stare at her in disbelief.

"It's why nobody is allowed to do overnights at Shadow Lake anymore. The person...or thing that did this is still out there in the woods."

The loudest crack of thunder yet booms from the sky so loud it sounds like it's right above us, with lightning following directly behind it. We all jump a little, then try to play it cool like we aren't scared. We just sit in silence, listening to the slowing raindrops hit the roof of our cabin, and think about how close we came to a murderer. Or a murderous beast. Within a minute or so, we hear a clicking sound and all the lights turn back on. Sarah's alarm clock is flashing 12:00 from her nightstand.

I look around the circle at the faces of the other girls and they are all pale, specifically the ones who were there that night. We are all thinking of the noise we heard and how it was probably one of the men screaming in terror from whatever was taking his life. Chills run up my arms at the thought.

"Alright, I'm just fucking with you guys. I had to come up with something to keep you entertained while the power was out. Okay, let's all head to the latrines and get ready for the real lights out," Sarah claps her hands together and hops to her feet so nonchalantly, I could scream.

"What? What do you mean? What happened to the men?" asks Trishelle.

"Who knows, they probably were long gone by the time we arrived."

"But, if nothing happened at Shadow Lake, why isn't anyone doing their overnight there this week?" pleads Rachel.

"It flooded last week after that big storm. Should be dried up by the next round of campers," Sarah answers, reaching up on her tiptoes to grab several items from the shelf above her bed. She tosses a toothbrush, bottle of meds, and some dental floss in her small travel bag and walks across the cabin.

None of us move. We are all stunned.

"You fucking got us all," mumbles Cassie.

"Language," Sarah winks on her way out the door, tapping above the door frame like she always does.

Within seconds, we are all in tears. We are laughing so hard our sides ache. We are laughing from relief that the story wasn't real, that the lights are back on, that there's nothing to be afraid of. We are laughing because she truly got us. Ten skeptical teenagers who doubt everything. She fucking got us.

I mindlessly find myself walking to the latrines with Cassie and her crew, still giggling over the joke. Cassie forgot her Seabreeze astringent, so I hand her mine with an extra cotton ball I fished out of my toiletries bag. It's moments like these that I wonder if Cassie is actually as horrible as we all think, or if she is simply playing a character. Maybe she enjoys living up to her horrible reputation as a spoiled brat. Maybe, just maybe, she isn't so bad after all.

I'll have to tell Jessie all about this when I write to her tonight.

Eighteen

The unthinkable has happened. Sarah and Pat have somehow convinced Dave to approve a co-ed nature hike. The girls of B-1 and the boys of A-1 will spend the next few hours hiking through the forest, learning about nature, and having a campfire cookout before turning around to head back to camp in time for quiet hour. This is unprecedented. Dave is so lost in the chaos of running Shady Oaks, I honestly don't think he has connected the dots and realized that Sarah and Pat are an item. It's wonderful.

I can't believe our luck as we stand behind the back doors of the kitchen and pack our crates and coolers with supplies and realize the boys are carrying everything. All I have to hold is my canteen filled with drinking water and, of course, my disposable camera.

We begin our hike down the long gravel drive, out to the camp entrance. Once we are outside the gates, Pat tells us we will have to walk single file on the side of the road for a quarter mile before we reach the entrance to the trail. A few cars pass us, and it's a stark reminder that there is life outside Shady Oaks. Families driving to the grocery store or the movie theater for a matinee. Young couples enjoying a carefree afternoon drive. I feel so isolated inside the gates for these two weeks; it's easy to forget that the rest of the world is still moving as it should.

Aiden is waiting for me at the trail head, as the path is wide enough for us to walk side-by-side. I'm floating. Surprisingly, Cassie and Vinny are walking in front of us, and he seems to be tolerating her. The entire premise of this nature hike was to teach us about…well, nature, but Sarah and Pat seem lost in their own world at the head of the pack and none of us care to change that. It's so fun getting to do an activity with the boys cabin; it feels forbidden. The energy is electric; everyone is smiling, mindlessly chatting, and enjoying the mid-afternoon sun. The trail is an easy hike but still scenic with its twists, turns, and changing foliage as we travel further into the woods.

Aiden and I have the time to talk more than we ever have, and it's wonderful. He occasionally pauses to readjust the bag of cooking supplies he has over his shoulder, and I can tell the weight is beginning to get to him.

"Do you want me to carry it for a minute?" I offer. He simply laughs and continues his story. He's telling me all about his first year at Menominee and how everyone treated him with skepticism when he arrived as an outsider, so he had to prove himself on the football field to gain respect. He is expected to make the varsity team this year as a sophomore, which is unheard of in the district. I can't imagine telling my friends that I'm dating a varsity football star. Who would have thought? Not me!

As the front of the line begins arriving at the campsite clearing, I can hear them drop the crates and bags they've been carrying around the firepit with varying thuds. Temperatures in the mid-eighties might not mean a lot for the rest of the country, but they can be pretty brutal in northern Michigan where we aren't accustomed to the heat. I'll never forget when one of my classmates moved to Gladstone from Arizona and learned that none of us have air conditioning units in our homes. *What is this, 1950?!*

I reach up to scratch the back of my neck where some sort of insect has bitten me, and my skin is red hot from being exposed during the hike. Apparently, this is still not the year I'm going to learn to apply sunscreen.

"Ladies and gentlemen, please follow us down to the water, we have a surprise for you!" yells Pat, who then looks to Sarah and winks. Oh, she's smitten.

All of us are sitting on logs around the firepit or leaning on trees in the shade, drinking out of our canteens and catching our breath from the hike.

"Come on, you're going to love it!" Sarah claps.

We all reluctantly start moving down the remainder of the trail to the water, which can barely be seen through the trees. I stay a few feet from Aiden as I discreetly sniff my underarms to make sure I don't have body odor from the hike. Luckily, the four coats of Teen Spirit deodorant that I lathered on seems to be doing its job.

When we make it to the sand beach, there are eleven canoes flipped over and pulled up in the sand, each with two orange life jackets leaned up against them.

"Surprise, everyone! We are going to use all the paddling skills you've been working on during lessons this week and go on a canoe trip!" yells Sarah.

"There's a small river that loops around off the edge of the lake. It will take about an hour to complete, and then we will come back here and cook some burgers!" adds Pat with his signature fist pump.

Everyone is nodding and looking to each other to choose partners. I'm not incredibly comfortable in a canoe yet, but I'm sure I'll get the hang of it. I grab one of the life jackets and loop it around the back of my neck. Before I can attach the white belt in front of me, Aiden is there to help.

"You look adorable. This is going to be fun," he whispers with a smile, before reaching down to grab his own life jacket and flipping the canoe over. "I'll hold onto the end of the boat, and you climb in. Remember to stay low. I'll push us off."

This is so much easier than when I got partnered with Cassie yesterday back at camp and she made me do all the work and then nearly drowned me for sport.

He pushes the canoe slightly into the water, holds it between his knees, and crosses his golden, toned arms to hold it in place. Aiden's chestnut hair is falling into his eyes while he holds the canoe for me to enter. I reach forward and brush it away for him; he smiles. I can hear giggling across the beach; everyone is having a hard time getting in without tipping their canoes over and the laughing is making their coordination even worse. I hear a scream directly next to us and stop in place to see what's going on. Cassie

128

has jumped out of the canoe and into the knee-deep water and is rapidly dusting herself off with both hands.

"Calm down, Cass, it's fine, I've got it," Vinny is assuring her.

"It was a tarantula!" she screams.

"Hey, hey, hey, it's fine; we don't even have tarantulas here. It was just a friendly spider. They are essential to nature. They are our friends," says Pat, calmly approaching Cassie with both hands up like a hostage negotiator.

I also have arachnophobia, but Cassie is physically shaking. I've never seen a reaction like this to a harmless spider.

"Just make sure it's gone. Please. I can't get back in that canoe until you check it," she says to Pat with doe eyes.

Sarah appears annoyed.

Both Pat and Vinny tip the canoe upside down, shake it out, and check all the nooks and crannies.

"All clear, princess," Vinny assures her, his tone dry and impatient.

She rolls her eyes and reluctantly takes position to board the canoe again. We all continue the process of launching into the lake, and I know I'm not the only girl silently scanning the bottom of the boat to check for eight-legged, unwanted visitors.

We all manage to glide deep enough to start paddling and it is hilarious to watch the other teams, which are mostly co-ed, try to communicate with each other enough to successfully steer their vessels in the right direction. Aiden and I are laughing so hard, I can feel the canoe shaking. The lake is empty today, with the exception of a few birds occasionally swooping down to skim the surface in a quest for food.

Aiden's calm voice directs me, barely above a whisper, when he needs me to paddle. We glide effortlessly to the front of the crowd, right behind Sarah and Pat. Some of the other teams are paddling in circles behind us, growing increasingly frustrated with their partners. I turn my head back to look at Aiden and he is smiling at me. There isn't a cloud in the sky.

Within minutes, the lake is narrowing into what Pat referred to as "the river," but I see it's more of a skinny lagoon that loops around by some modest vacation homes, before emptying back out on the other side of the lake. I'm thankful to see this, as my visions of rapids didn't align with the skills of my fellow campers. As the cove narrows, there is a small current, but it's more of an accelerant for the canoes to pass around the corner than a hazard.

Or so I thought.

Screams followed by two splashes sound from behind us. Before I can turn to see what happened, Sarah yells, "Everyone, grab onto something near the shore to hold your canoe in place while we get these campers right side up!"

Sarah and Pat turn their canoe around, furiously paddling against the mild current to get to the campers. I turn around and Aiden points to a tree with long, wiry branches growing over the edge of the water to our right. "Grab on," he shouts.

We stop paddling and float towards the tree, until we are close enough to grab onto the branches. We barely slow our pace enough to catch on, nearly passing right by. I laugh as I struggle to reach up and grip the branch above me. When he does the same with a larger branch, the whole tree shakes. I steady myself and turn around to see who it was that fell out of their canoe. I'm not too concerned; the water isn't that deep, and everyone is wearing a life jacket. I imagine it will be more of an inconvenience than anything. I'm straining my eyes to recognize the floating heads in the water; it's Trishelle and Rachel. I'm convinced the biggest tragedy of the day will be that they have wet hair in front of the boys.

Something tickles my right ear and I reach up to swat it away, only to feel it again on my left leg. I turn back around to face forward and freeze. There are two spiders that look like daddy longlegs in the boat in front of me. I don't know what to do. I feel another tickle on my shoulder and brush it off immediately. It's another spider. I quickly realize they are coming from the tree above us; we must have disturbed them when we grabbed onto the branches. Another falls and hits my thigh and I completely panic. I don't scream; I can't form a sound. Without much thought, I jump out of the canoe, but the motion I create by kicking my legs knocks Aiden out, too. I want to apologize, but I'm stricken with terror. Spiders are continuing to drop out of the tree. I swim away, as fast as my arms will take me. I unsnap my life jacket so I can submerge my whole body under water. I need to make sure they aren't in my hair or under my shirt. My chest feels tight. I'm quietly gasping for breath, willing my heart to slow down.

When I begin to regain my senses, I see Aiden has flipped the canoe upside down and is dragging it toward me by the rope tied to the front. I didn't even realize at this point I am standing on the bottom of the lake; the water is only up to my shoulders. Aiden wades through the water with soaking wet hair, and I'm mortified. I didn't think about him at all when I jumped out of that boat and knocked him over in the process. He might be furious, and rightfully so.

He walks directly in front of me, loops the rope around his arm so the canoe won't float away, and puts both hands on my shoulders, just like the first day we met. He's inspecting me to make sure I'm okay, also like the first day we met.

He looks me in the eyes, and I can see him attempting to gauge my mental state.

"They are all gone, they are nowhere near you. That was my fault, I should have known better than to grab onto that tree so hard. It's going to be okay. Let's breathe," he calmly dictates and begins to take deep breaths for me to mimic.

"Let's walk over to the other edge, I'm going to check the boat over to make sure they are all gone," he says and leads me over to the bank, where I put my life jacket back on and fix my water-logged ponytail.

The rest of the group is now catching up; they must have stopped well behind us when Trishelle and Rachel went in. They all slowly pass us, smiling because they think we simply fell in the water as well.

Aiden helps me climb back into the canoe and all I can think about is how calm he kept me during one of the most terrible moments of my life and how safe I felt with him by my side. This must be what love feels like.

When we get back to the campsite, I throw my life jacket off, still feeling the itch all over my body. Aiden sees the discomfort and checks me, once again, for spiders.

"Let's get a fire built. We'll put you close enough to the flames; it will chase off any of those pesky daddy longlegs that dare get near you again."

I roll my eyes and grab my rolled-up towel from the sand. I'm shaking from the cold and I'm not sure I've ever been so hungry. Pat is standing on land, helping campers out of their canoes when Vinny pulls up with Cassie at the head of the boat. As the tip of the canoe gets safely lodged in the sand, Pat reaches his hand out for Cassie, and she stumbles forward into his arms.

"Whoa there," he says as he catches her.

Cassie remains holding onto Pat's shoulders and looks up into his eyes. He is obviously uncomfortable, and she appears as if she might kiss him.

"You saved my life," she coos, giving him a wink before letting go and stepping into the sand. Vinny and Sarah both appear to be less-than-thrilled. I'm not sure if Cassie does these things for attention or simply for the thrill. I can't wait to write about this whole afternoon in a letter tonight to Jess.

We, as a group, build a bonfire and it roars within minutes, warming our wet skin. Pat volunteers the boys to cook our lunches, so each one of them is cooking two burgers over the fire. I laugh as Vinny carelessly slaps mayonnaise all over Cassie's bun while she berates him about the calorie content.

I'm distracted by the absence of Sarah and Pat, who haven't spoken to each other since Cassie's flirtatious episode down at the lake. When they reemerge from the woods, Sarah's eyes are red and I seem to be the only one who even noticed they were gone.

"I've got a very important question to ask you," Aiden says, peeling back the tinfoil to check on our meals.

I tilt my head towards him and scrunch my nose.

He smiles.

"How do you take your burger?"

Nineteen

Now

"So, you're really going? I'm proud of you!"

I balance the phone between my ear and shoulder as I hold a few outfits up in the mirror before throwing them in my suitcase.

"I haven't dressed to leave the house in a while. I wouldn't be too proud until you see what I'm packing," I respond.

Jessie laughs. "Whatever amount of sweatpants you have packed for this three-day journey two miles from your house, please reduce it by three."

I look at the four pairs of sweatpants in assorted shades of gray rolled up in my bag and smile. If I'm going out of my comfort zone to attend this reunion, I can at least sleep comfortably.

"I still can't believe I'm doing this without you."

I can hear a gate agent making a boarding announcement in the background.

"Trust me, I know. But I just landed in Detroit, and I can't miss this conference. I'm so sorry, Q. I can't wait to hear all about it when I get back Tuesday."

I glance over at my blank notebook sitting on the vanity in the corner of my room. I walk over and toss it into my luggage.

"I'm going to write down everything notable that happens, just like we used to," I promise her.

I can feel her smiling on the other end of the phone.

"Ha, I almost forgot. Yes, every detail, I want to hear it all," she says.

After hanging up, I wander into my walk-in closet to find something presentable to wear for the dance, which the invitation states will be on Sunday night. I have countless dresses leftover from the events I used to attend when I first hit the bestseller list. I don't think I turned down a single invitation for the first two years of my success as a writer.

There is a shoebox on the top shelf, and I climb up my step ladder to retrieve it. I nearly tumble off when I open the lid. It's all my old pictures from Shady Oaks. They are still enclosed in paper envelopes from getting them developed at Shopko each summer after returning home from camp. I climb down and sit cross legged on the floor of my closet as I begin to flip through the memories I haven't seen in years. I laugh out loud when I see that the first picture in the stack is from shortly after arrival that first summer; I had snapped a quick picture of the activity courts as Jessie and I were approaching them. You can see Aiden, Vinny, and two other boys I don't recognize playing volleyball in the distance. This must have been about thirty seconds before I got nailed in the face.

There are pictures from our first overnight, Jessie posing proudly next to the tent she assembled. There is one from arts and crafts of Jessie and I holding up our painted rocks. The first one in the next stack is of Aiden, still soaked from our canoe incident, cooking my burger in a pan over our midday campfire after returning to the site.

"And what are we doing in here?" asks Randall, leaning in the door frame to my closet with his apron slung over his shoulder.

"How are you still here? I told you to take some time off," I smile, knowing Randall always needs to be forced to take time off. "I'm looking at pictures from camp, want to join me?"

He smiles.

"I spent eighteen years in the closet, I don't care to go back in. Also, the reason I'm still here is because I portioned up some meals, so in the event that you come home early, you don't starve to death. I don't need that on my conscience"

"Oh, shut up and get over here," I laugh, and he sits down next to me. I'm still holding the picture of Aiden next to the fire.

"Is *that* Aiden? I understand why you acted like such a love-struck little puppy, sheesh!"

I take a minute to appreciate how handsome he was at such a young age. He's gotten even better looking somehow. I quickly flip it to the back with its duplicate to reveal the next photo in the stack.

"Wait, why are there two of every picture?" asks Randall.

"God, you're so young. Well, my dear Randall, back in the nineteen-hundreds, we used to bring our cameras to the store to get developed. There was a little box you could check to get two of every picture so you could share them with your friends."

Randall rolls his eyes and grabs another stack of photos; these ones are placed in a plastic bag that I recognize. My heart rate instantly elevates.

He pulls them out of the bag and begins to flip through. I see flashes of a dark beach, shoes in the sand, and toes in the water.

"Well, why doesn't this stack have duplicates?" he asks.

I gently take the stack from his hands and flip them face down. It's been decades and I'm still not ready to look at them.

"Because the police are still holding them for evidence."

Twenty

Then

Last year, I felt a burst of excitement on the last morning of camp. I had naïve optimism that I'd see Aiden in the winter, and I couldn't wait to get back to Gladstone and tell my friends about him. Today, I'm grieving. He gets his license in January and I won't have mine until March. Neither of our parents are going to let us make the one-hour journey in the snow unsupervised, which means we most likely won't see each other until late spring.

It's a Shady Oaks tradition to sing "Come Saturday Morning" by the Sandpipers at our last breakfast and, what was once simply a sappy song of yesteryear is now the soundtrack to my broken heart. *We'll travel for smiles in our Saturday smiles and then we'll move on. But we will remember, long after Saturday's gone.* I quickly wipe my eyes so nobody will see the tears forming at their edges.

I've barely touched my breakfast as we listen to Dave make his annual end-of-camp announcements after the last song. Aiden and his friends are sitting at the table behind Jessie and I and they are turned around to face Dave while he speaks. Aiden has his knees propped up so I can lean back against them. It's the most PDA we can get away with, without getting scolded by the other counselors in the mess hall.

The staff performs an offbeat musical number they wrote to commemorate Shady Oak's 40th anniversary. Even Marge joins in, waving her hands in the air with the rest of the kitchen staff. The janitors crack a rare smile as they stand in the doorway and watch. After the song is over, Dave announces that he would like us to join him in welcoming some members of Shady Oak's inaugural summer from 1958. He motions for us all to stand and give them a round of applause. My view is obstructed by all the campers who tower over me until we are seated again. When I scan the seven adults who have entered the room, I'm surprised they aren't elderly like I anticipated. I quickly do the math in my head and realize they are most likely only in their fifties. I'm not sure why I was envisioning walking canes.

Over the next twenty minutes, they tell us stories of what it was like to be the first campers to stay at Shady Oaks. Back then, campers stayed for an entire month. There were outhouses and outdoor showers, both of which would result in countless mosquito bites. The now-abandoned cabins were built in the early 1960s; the first few years they slept in giant tents for the entire month. They also had mandatory Shady Oaks uniforms, consisting of t-shirts with the camp's logo, terrycloth shorts, and knee-high socks. We are all mesmerized by the stories of how life used to be. Before they leave, Dave says that we have time for a few questions. The entire camp seems to raise their hands at once.

"Did you know Timothy?" shouts a camper from across the mess hall.

All seven of the adults look to each other uncomfortably.

"Yes, we did," answers one of the men. Nobody elaborates.

"Well, are the stories true?" shouts another camper.

"Okay, let's go ahead and give these folks a round of applause for traveling all this way to speak to us today," Dave cuts in.

Nobody moves.

"No," says Jack, the janitor who had the restroom run-in with Cassie last year. He steps forward, towards the group in the middle of the mess hall. One of the women reaches her hand up and rubs his forearm with pain in her downcast eyes. I know I'm not alone in my confusion.

"Timothy was my older brother."

Gasps echo throughout the room and the adults circle around behind Jack in a show of support.

"I started working here so I could feel closer to 'em. Our parents are gone now, and this place holds the last memories I have of Timothy. Somewhere over the years, my brother's story changed from a tragedy to a ghost story...a punchline...an urban legend."

Dave's face is white.

"Jack, we had no idea you were his brother. We would have never made light of the situation, we were just trying to have fun with the campers," he pleads.

"No, Dave, 'yer a good man and ya have nothing to apologize for. Everyone loves a good ghost story, me included. I just want yas all to remember that the story of Timothy exists because a boy died. He died in that lake and our parents took their last breaths without gettin' any answers."

Twenty-One

Spring of 1999 seemed to take years to arrive. Winter was cold, dark, and long. I reluctantly went to the Homecoming dance with my neighbor, Ben Boyer, so that I didn't have to show up alone. I spent the entirety of the night sipping over-sugared punch and wishing Aiden could have come.

Jessie stayed the weekend with me twice, both times dad had to go pick her up because her parents were face down from a morning full of whiskey by noon. I appreciated the effort my father put into making the visits as normal as possible for her. We had dinner, he dropped us off at the movie theater or the mall, we even went ice skating. The sadness in her eyes when Sunday mornings came around will stay with me forever.

In late February, a miracle came in the form of my brother falling in love with a girl from Marinette, which is the town neighboring Menominee, where Aiden and Vinny live. With some mild begging and pleading, I not only convinced dad to let me go on a trip to visit with Matt, but I also talked Matt into taking Jessie with us. She had just broken things off with Jake (or the other way around, I'm not sure I got the complete story) and was happy to accompany me to watch one of Vinny's basketball games with Aiden.

"Look, I'm dropping you girls off at the school and I'll be back to pick you up at the end of the game. Not a minute later," Matt tells us as he's carefully buckling a vase full of roses for his *girlfriend* in the backseat.

"Okay, *dad*," I reply, and this gets a laugh out of Jessie, who is sitting in the backseat, next to the flowers.

"You two little shits are lucky I'm letting you tag along on this trip. Don't push it."

I look up to the rearview mirror and catch Jessie's gaze. We are both smiling.

The trip takes a little over an hour from our house to the Menominee High School gym. Although it's a rare sunny day in winter, there is still a foot or two of snow on the ground, so Matt drives the speed limit and keeps his death metal music at an acceptable volume. He pulls up in front of the school to let us out, and my anxiety goes into overdrive. I can't believe we are here. Aiden said he'd meet us inside the doors, but I begin to panic that maybe there are several sets of doors, and we won't find him before the game starts.

"I'll be outside at 8pm, please don't make me have to get out and come look for you," Matt warns us.

"We won't," we both promise in unison.

We walk through the heavy double doors in front of the gym and are greeted by two girls around our age, sitting at a folding table with a cash box in front of them.

"How many?" one of the girls asks. I look at Jessie. I think we have ten dollars between the two of us, I never thought about having to buy tickets. Just as I'm about to ask how much they are, Aiden pops his head around the corner.

"Kim, they're with me," he smiles and nods to Jessie and me.

Kim blushes and says, "Of course. Go right in!"

We thank her and I walk past the table to greet Aiden with a hug.

"You're blonde!" I shriek.

"I know," he smiles bashfully and raises his fingers to touch the frosted tips of his hair. His haircut is also an inch or so shorter than it was last summer. "What do you think?"

"I love it," I lie. Although it's not the color I would have chosen for him, he'd be handsome enough to pull off purple hair if he wanted.

He greets Jessie with a quick embrace and asks about Jake.

"Don't even ask," she responds with an eye roll.

"Fair enough, let's grab some popcorn for the game. Vinny was so stoked when I told him you guys were coming."

Aiden walks us over to a concession stand outside the entrance doors to the gym. There is an older couple working the stand, and they are both incredibly tan, which is an indication of financial stability this time of year – it means they can afford to escape the cold. Aiden puts his hand behind my back and gently nudges me forward towards the woman, who has the warmest smile. I look at Aiden and tell him I'm not quite sure what I want and that I'll just split something with him, his choice. The man finishes topping off a hot dog for the customer before us and turns his focus on Aiden and I. He is smiling as well. Everyone in Menominee seems so friendly.

"Mom, dad, I'd like you to meet Quinn," Aiden says and holds his arms out like he's displaying a prize on The Price is Right.

I chuckle.

I quickly realize he's not joking.

"Mom and dad?" I ask, panicked. I hear Jessie choke out a surprised laugh. The woman lifts the gate that separates them from the line of customers and comes around to us, followed by the man.

"Quinn! Aiden has been telling us all about you. We are so glad you could make it! You are just a doll," she sweetly exclaims, before wrapping me in a hug. She also hugs Jessie, who is smiling so hard at this awkward situation I'm in, I think her cheeks might bust open. His father also hugs me and pats Aiden on the back. I could die.

"Mr. and Mrs. Brooks, I didn't realize I'd be meeting you today. It's such a pleasure," I say in my most polite tone. I'm reconsidering everything: my hair, my outfit, all my life choices before this moment.

"Oh, please, call us Rose and Glenn!" his mother says with a warm smile while rubbing my arm.

Five minutes later, we are finding open seats on the bench with our arms full of snacks and pop, none of which we had to pay for. Jessie is still laughing so hard at what happened, her mascara is pooling at the corners of her eyes.

"I could kill you," I say to Aiden as soon as we take our seats.

"If I told you that they'd be here, you wouldn't have come. Or, you would have, but you'd have stressed yourself sick about it. This was the most logical way to introduce you," he says while casually throwing a kernel of popcorn in his mouth and taking a sip of his Pepsi.

"God, you know her so well," Jessie says, wiping her eyes with a cheap brown napkin from the concession stand.

Aiden winks at me and we all stand for the national anthem. I cannot believe that introducing me to his parents was a completely routine, stress-free event for him.

After we sit down, the starting lineup for the Menominee Maroons is announced and the crowd goes wild for their starting point guard, Vinny Brooks. Aiden is hooting and hollering for his cousin, and it makes me appreciate how tightknit their family is.

"I don't remember him being so good looking," Jessie leans over to whisper in my ear.

"You're single now, that's why," I respond.

"So is he," Aiden says with a wink, overhearing our conversation.

Throughout the game, several of Aiden's classmates stop by to introduce themselves, and I've never felt so important.

"We all have posters of Britney Spears in our lockers, but Aiden has a picture of *Quinn from Gladstone*. Trust me, we've all given him shit about it," says one friend, also sporting frosted blonde tips at the end of his brunette hair. The band 98 Degrees started this trend, and they should also be responsible for ending it.

The Maroons defeat the Ishpeming Hematites by one point when Vinny nails a shot at the buzzer. I don't even like basketball, yet I'm on my feet screaming with the rest of the fans in the bleachers. What a feeling. Maybe I should start following sports.

We all rush the court to congratulate the team and it's a scene from an after-school movie. Everyone is high-fiving, hugging, celebrating. Aiden's parents embrace Vinny and introduce Jessie and I to Vinny's parents. They invite us to join the family at Big Boy for a celebratory meal. I tell them about my brother Matt and how he'll never allow it.

"How old is he?" asks Vinny's dad.

"Twenty-two," I answer, and they both look at each other and smile.

"We'll handle him," answers Glenn, Aiden's dad.

Matt pulls up in his Honda Civic and does a double take when he sees the adults Jessie and I are standing outside with. We've only been waiting for two minutes, but we're already shivering, and a light snow has begun to fall.

Glenn and Vinny Sr. walk to Matt's side of the car and motion for him to roll his window down. They lean in and say something to him; within seconds I hear boisterous laughter. All three are smiling and the two dads motion for Jessie and I to get in Matt's car. Aiden and Vinny fist bump.

"We'll meet you at Big Boy," Glenn says.

As we walk past them to get in the car, Vinny Sr. whispers to me, "One thing about twenty-two-year-old boys, they'll do anything for a free meal." He pats me on the back with a smile and continues to the parking lot.

Jessie and I are overcome with emotion.

"You are the coolest brother ever," she tells Matt as we get buckled in.

After a quick call from the payphone outside the restaurant to smooth dad over, my curfew is extended by an hour, and we have time to enjoy dinner with the extended Brooks family.

We get a big table in a private room in the back that seats all nine of us. We raise our red plastic cups filled with soft drinks to toast to Vinny, the star of the game. I order the slim jim, which was mom's favorite thing to order at the Big Boy twenty minutes from our home in Gladstone. It makes me smile and wonder what she'd think of this scene. I know she'd love Aiden. She'd be proud of Matt for being generous and driving Jessie and I tonight. I wish things were different; she could fit right in at the empty chair next to Matt. I wish she knew what she was missing.

Vinny's mom asks Matt about the girl he's seeing in Marinette, and they actually know her family from church. We talk about Shady Oaks, we talk about Matt's work, we talk about college plans. We laugh and nobody argues. This scene would fit in one of the shows in the TGIF lineup on ABC.

Aiden's parents grab the check and pay for everyone's meals. They don't even discuss it; his mom just pulls cash out of her billfold, hands it to the waiter, and tells him to keep the change. When we dine out with our extended family once a year for grandma's birthday, my Uncle Roger gets a calculator out and charges every family member to the penny for their meals before anyone is allowed to leave.

"Quinn, we are overjoyed that we finally got to meet the girl Aiden has gone on and on about. We hope we'll get to meet your father at Shady Oaks drop off this year," his mother tells me, holding both of my hands in hers.

"I'm sure he'd love that," I answer, wondering how or when I'm going to break the news of Aiden to dad. He is under the impression that we went to Menominee tonight because they were playing my high school, Gladstone.

We are getting in Matt's car to leave when Vinny runs up and knocks on Jessie's window. She quickly rolls it down.

"I wanted to ask if you have AOL Instant Messenger," Vinny says with a smile.

"I just got it," Jessie responds.

Vinny extends his hand through the open window and hands Jessie a napkin and pen to write down her username.

"Let's keep in touch."

Twenty-two

Now

Aiden asked me to come to the reunion an hour before everyone else is scheduled to arrive so he could give me a private tour. I gladly obliged. I can't tell you the last time I've driven a car, but two miles down an empty backroad doesn't take much skill, so I'm managing fine.

When I pull in, Aiden is talking to an older man with a clipboard, pointing to something in the distance. He smiles, waves, and directs me to a spot on the grass.

"Quinn Harstead, it's a pleasure to have you back," says the man. I can't place his name. He leans forward to shake my hand and I take note of his legs.

"Dave!" I exclaim. "How are you?"

"Life's been good, but I'm so happy to finally be back where I belong," he answers.

"Dave, I'm going to show her around, but I'll be back up here before the other campers arrive," Aiden shakes his hand and turns to grab my bag. "Quinn, let me show you to your bunk."

We walk slowly through the turf-like green grass and I can't focus my eyes on just one thing; there's so much to see. I look through the windows of the arts and crafts cabin to see a dozen easels set up, fully stocked with paint. The mess hall has a fresh coat of stain on its wooden exterior and there has been a patio built on the back end. There is a picnic table with an umbrella on a concrete pad outside the back door.

"For Marge's smoke breaks," Aiden says, shaking his head. "She's beside herself with emotion over the changes. I installed a new double oven and she hugged me so tightly, I thought she broke one of my ribs."

As if on cue, Marge peaks her head out the back door of the hall and waves to us. A cigarette is hanging from the corner of her cracked lips and a kitchen towel out of her back pocket. If it weren't for the deepened creases on her face, I'd think no time had gone by at all.

"So, you're showing me to my bunk? And where will that be?"

"Well, Miss Harstead, here at Shady Oaks, the boys and girls stay in separate cabins. Nineteen females RSVP'd, so I split the group of you among the cabins so you can let me know if anything needs attention before the paying campers arrive next weekend."

"Well, Mr. Brooks, I sure appreciate your hospitality," I answer and nudge him with my elbow. We continue walking towards the waterfront and I smile when I pass B-2; my first cabin at Shady Oaks. He doesn't slow down, so I know exactly where we are headed: B-1.

We stop in front of the screen door, and I can hardly catch my breath. Flashes of memories flood my thoughts. The last time I saw this cabin, dad was hurriedly throwing my belongings into my suitcase and ushering me out the door and into his truck. I didn't even take the time to look back and say goodbye. Aiden doesn't seem to recognize how much it's affecting me. He leans forward and holds the door open with a bright smile, excited to show me the improvements. I grin and breathe deeply as I cross the threshold.

"Oh, Aiden," I whisper.

It's beautiful. All the floors have been refinished. I can smell the fresh cedar wall panels. The windows and doors have been replaced. There are locks on the handles now, where there had never been before. I note that there are locks on the interior of the windows as well. I hear something electrical click on, and my attention goes to the far wall, where there is a brand-new air-conditioning unit installed.

"You've got to be kidding me," I laugh.

"Hey, it's hard enough to get these damn kids to give up their cellphones. There's no way they'll go without cold air."

I roll my eyes and shake my head in disbelief. Air conditioning units at Camp Shady Oaks.

I choose my bed, which is in the same location as the last year I attended, but the mattress and frame have been replaced with a much higher quality set. Every bed in the room is already made with sheets and matching fluffy, red plaid comforters.

I throw my suitcase down on the floor next to the bed.

"Can I show you the rest before everyone else gets here?" Aiden asks.

I'd love to stay in this cabin and kiss the man I've been thinking of for the last twenty-three years, but things are still at the cordial stage between us. It's been so long since I've kissed a man, I wouldn't even know where to begin.

We walk out of the cabin and towards the waterfront. There are poles along the way with twinkly lights strung between them, which will illuminate the path at night.

"Solar," Aiden points at the small panels on each pole. Times sure have changed.

We reach the waterfront and I'm again rendered speechless. This place holds memories on every level of my emotional spectrum. I remember Aiden playing with my hair that second summer while we watched the counselors perform their silly chants. I remember learning to tread water and thinking I'd never make it longer than a few minutes. I remember that glorious final summer when I tested high enough to be on the scuba diving crew. I remember getting my heart broken on this very path. I remember the last night of summer camp in 1999, when all our lives changed in an instant.

Twenty-three

Then

What a bittersweet feeling it is to arrive for the first day of my last year of camp. So much anticipation, but also a creeping feeling in the back of my mind that I should cherish every moment because I'll never be here again.

I reluctantly told dad about Aiden on the drive to camp today. I was behind the wheel of his truck, so there was no turning around once he knew. He handled it a lot better than expected. He even agreed to meet his parents at drop off.

"Just please," I begin, before he cuts me off.

"Just please nothing, Quinn. I'm a grown man and you don't have to constantly tell me how I should act in front of other grown adults."

I breathe deeply, putting the scenario of a peaceful encounter out in the universe. I learned about the power of positivity recently and I'm trying my best.

"Yes sir."

"You know, I do see the phone bill. I'm not a complete idiot," he says, and I can feel him look over at me from the corner of my eye.

The remainder of the drive is spent in silence, with dad raising his hands ever so subtly each time he thinks I need to slow my speed or brake a little easier. He'll never really get used to me being old enough to drive.

"That's them," I say as we pull up to camp, pointing to Mr. Brooks' silver Audi.

"Well, la-ti-da," dad responds with his pinky in the air.

"*Dad*," I say through gritted teeth.

"Okay, okay."

I get out of the truck and give Aiden (who grew the blonde out of his hair, thank God) a quick side hug and turn to give Vinny the same. Aiden's parents warmly greet me and then turn towards dad with their hands extended to greet him.

He is polite and decent, rambling on with the usual pleasantries exchanged in an introduction like this. I'm impressed and relieved. Dad then turns to Aiden and Vinny.

"And which one of you young men are gambling with your lives by dating my only daughter?"

"*Dad*," I plead once again.

His stern gaze slowly transforms into a smile that only I can see through.

"Only kidding, boys," he says, both palms up in defense.

Aiden steps forward to shake his hand.

"I'm Aiden, sir. I believe we've spoken briefly on the phone when I've called for Quinn. This is my cousin, Vinny."

Dad chuckles.

"Huh – two yoots."

The four of us erupt in laughter.

"Quinn said the same thing when we met," Aiden smiles.

"Look out for my Quinnie and you and I will get along just fine," dad says, shaking Aiden's hand, who nods in response.

Dad pats me on the back and returns to the bed of his truck to unload my bags. The goodbye this year is much easier than the last. Neither Aiden nor Vinny's parents insist on walking them to their cabins, either. We all say goodbye to our families and are left standing in the patch of grass outside the mess hall with our suitcases as the vehicles pull away. This is it, our final year at Shady Oaks.

"Finally!"

I turn to see Jessie approaching us, her beautiful blonde hair fluttering in the wind. She got her braces off last month and I motion for her to smile and show me.

"Okay, supermodel!" I laugh as I embrace her.

"They look perfect," adds Vinny.

He approaches her and there is an awkwardness in the air. I know they've been speaking on Instant Messenger for months but have yet to see each other in person again until now.

"Thank you," she responds, tucking a few loose strands of hair behind her ear. "It's good to see you."

Vinny smiles like The Cheshire Cat.

"It's good to see you, too."

Jessie and I split off to check the newly installed bulletin board with cabin assignments outside the mess hall. Our welcome packets explained that there was a record number of fifteen and sixteen-year-olds registered for the summer of 1999, and some sessions would see the age groups split among two different cabins. We sent our registrations in together with a request to be housed in the same cabin. Luckily, it seems they listened.

"Finally, B-1!" shouts Jessie after finding our names on the list. "Oh my god."

"What?" I ask, scanning the list.

"Cassie isn't on it," Jessie whispers with wide eyes. She must be mistaken. I scan the list twice, three times. She's right. Cassie isn't in B-1. "This is going to be the best summer of our lives."

I'm still in disbelief as I scan the lists for the other cabins. There she is: B-2. She is going to be livid.

I look back at the top of our list and I nod my head after seeing *Sarah Lewis* in bold print at the top. I'll be in Sarah's cabin for the third year in a row. Jessie may just be right; this *is* going to be the best summer ever.

Twenty-four

The Scuba Divas. That's what they call us.

Jessie, Rachel, Trishelle, Cassie, and me. We are the five females who managed to pass out of the highest swim skills test and make it on the scuba crew. Much to my pleasure, the class is coed and Aiden, Vinny, and two other boys I hadn't met will be joining us for lessons every afternoon at 2pm. Several other kids also tested out of Level 5, but there is only one scuba instructor, so the leftover campers are going to take windsailing lessons with Pat.

I learn that Cassie and her sidekicks made the decision to send in their camp applications together as well, so they are all stuck in B-2. Their counselor? *Marge's niece.* What would my mom call this entire situation? *Serendipitous.* My only regret is that our shy little sidekick, Caroline, is stuck in there with those monsters. We'll have to give her refuge during meals to salvage her sanity. Jessie and I barely know the other girls in our cabin, and we don't mind at all. I'd rather be in a house full of strangers than sleeping next to Cassie Huntington.

The first day of scuba is amazing, if you ignore Cassie's complaints about the "used" mouthpieces we are "forced" to use and how one call to her father would remedy the situation. We all basically ignore her nonsense and direct our attention to Lena. We've all heard the horror stories of how you can *literally die* from scuba diving mistakes, so we soak in every word.

"The most important thing to remember is that oxygen tanks are not a toy. You are being trusted to follow my directions when in the water. This is serious business," Lena tells us while she sits on the dock, her tan legs kicking in the water below. We are all standing in waist-deep water, goosebumps covering our bodies from the unseasonably chilly afternoon. I'm trying to focus on anything other than how cold I am.

"Rule number one is to always have a buddy when you dive. After checking that your equipment is functioning and ready, your primary responsibility is to have eyes on your buddy so you can detect any signs of distress immediately."

"If we get the bends, will we die?" asks Rachel.

"Even at the deepest point, this lake is nowhere near the depth you'd have to dive for decompression sickness to be an issue," Lena responds. "What *can* happen in shallow water are lung expansion issues, which is why your manner and rate of breathing is so incredibly important."

As I listen to Lena's words, I'm regretting my excitement to join this class. To put it mildly, I'm terrified. I have a small sense of relief when Lena tells us that we won't actually be diving today; we are simply identifying the different pieces of equipment and learning how to put it all on when we are ready to dive. We won't be doing any underwater drills until the next day. My anxiety can subside for the next twenty-four hours.

When class is done, we all walk back up to the sand beach to retrieve our towels and coverups and change out of our water shoes and back into flip-flops. Aiden sits next to me on one of the log benches and I laugh as we both pull off our water shoes to expose our wrinkled toes.

"Put your feet up to mine and let me take a picture. This is what we are going to look like when we grow old and wrinkly," I say with a laugh.

He gladly obliges and I snap a quick photo.

As I'm putting my wet shoes into my beach bag and slipping on my Old Navy flip-flops, I hear Cassie walk by and whisper *bitch,* which gets uproarious laughter from Trishelle and Rachel. I turn around in confusion and realize the insult was directed at Jessie, who is sitting two rows behind us.

"Get a fucking life, Cassie," Vinny says as he exits the water and marches up the sand towards the benches.

"That's not what you said this winter," Cassie winks before continuing her walk up the path to her cabin.

Jessie is stunned silent, and Vinny looks panicked.

"I swear, Jess, I don't know what the fuck that crazy bitch is talking about."

I swing around to look at Aiden, but he simply shrugs his shoulders and pulls a white t-shirt over his head. I can't believe he wouldn't have told me if he knew Vinny and Cassie hooked up this winter. Surely,

161

she's just being the typical chaotic mess she always is and starting drama because Vinny rejected her.

I stand up and walk up to Jessie, grabbing her bag and wrapping my arm around hers. She still hasn't said a word.

"Let's go," I tell her.

"Wait," interjects Vinny.

I hold my palm up towards him and shake my head. I made a promise to myself that Jessie's well-being would be my priority and I don't intend to break that promise any time soon.

Twenty-five

Now

"I understand how tacky this is, but would you mind signing my book?"

I smile warmly at the woman who has just entered B-1, but I don't believe we've met before.

"It would be my pleasure," I answer, taking her well-read copy of *Summer of '99* and Sharpie, before leaning over on my bed to sign my name on the title page. "Did we go to camp together?"

She blushes and averts my gaze as she explains that she was only thirteen that last summer, so we didn't interact much.

"I obviously knew who you were because you were in the Scuba Divas, but we never actually talked. My name is Crystal," she says.

Scuba Divas. I haven't thought about that name in ages.

"Well, hopefully we can make up for lost time and get to know each other this weekend," I tell her. This gets a very enthusiastic smile.

"Could I also maybe get a quick picture? My book club is never going to believe this."

After approximately eleven attempts at the perfect shot to elicit envy from her friends, Crystal settles on a selfie with her and I next to the cabin door, holding three copies of my previous books, in which I have now signed personalized inscriptions for her. I haven't met with readers in years, and I forgot how mentally exhausting it can be. You want to be everything they hoped you would be: generous, kind, patient, and attentive. Trying to be all those things for everyone in a line of a hundred people is the mental equivalent of running a marathon. I got in the habit of scheduling two-hour naps after each signing event.

Luckily, we are interrupted by the screen door opening and I grin at a face I'd recognize anywhere: Caroline. Shy little Caroline. Although her facial features haven't changed at all in the last two decades, her confidence and style have had a complete overhaul. She looks like she stepped directly out of a J Crew catalog. When she sees me, she smiles, and I mentally calculate how much her smile must have cost. It's blindingly perfect.

"Well, I didn't know we were having celebrity guests!"

I smile and shake my head before meeting her inside the door for a hug.

"Caroline, you look stunning!"

"Well, I could say the same for you. I haven't seen your name in the news for a while, I was worried you were dead," she laughs.

"Not dead, just taking a break," I say with a forced smile.

Caroline chooses the bed next to mine and updates me on her life as she's hanging her clothes in the newly built mini closet with recessed lighting and a bronze clothing rod. There's one next to each bed in the cabin. Aiden really spared no expense.

Caroline lives in New York City and is a copywriter for a big fashion magazine. She is married to an architect, and they have two small children. I would have never in a million years predicted this path for her life. I'm incredibly happy for her. I wish I knew back then that everything would turn out just fine for the apprehensive little bookworm who sat quietly at our lunch table.

I let her and Crystal, who has been hanging on every word of our conversation, know that I'm going to step out for a little fresh air. Luckily, this turns Crystal's attention fully on Caroline and I can excuse myself easily.

I step outside the cabin and take a deep breath of fresh Michigan air, which always seems to smell just a little sweeter this time of year. There are a few birds singing in the trees next to the cabin and I can detect the scent of something cooking on charcoal outside the mess hall from here. It's amazing how smells like these can bring back childhood memories that are stored so deep, you nearly forgot they were there.

"Well, if it isn't my favorite camper."

I'm startled by the voice. I was so lost in my memories; I didn't hear anyone coming down the path.

I smile at the woman before me, carrying a garment bag over one arm and a duffle bag slung around her shoulder. She is wearing a head scarf and her skin is a pale shade of gray. The bags under her eyes make it seem like she hasn't slept in weeks and she's wearing a t-shirt about two sizes too big for her emaciated frame. I sense a familiarity in her face, but it doesn't click until she smiles.

"Sarah?"

She nods.

"I know, quite a shock to see me this way. I didn't plan on coming, but I couldn't miss the chance to see this place again before I go."

I tilt my head. "Before you go?"

Her lips curl into a sad smile and I know she's had to explain her situation more often than she'd like.

"Breast cancer. We caught it too late, and the treatments have become too hard on my body, so I'm letting go and accepting the inevitable."

A sob escapes my lips and I awkwardly cough to cover it up. I can't tell you the last time I've cried, yet I'm immediately devastated over this news from a woman I haven't seen in decades. Even though this place holds a lot of heartache, it also is the source of a lot of happy memories in my life and she's a primary reason. I loved every minute spent with Sarah. She was kind, she was fun, she was fair. She was fully dedicated to making the camp experience wonderful for us. The world needs more people like her, not less. I walk down the stairs from the cabin and stand before her.

"I am so sorry, Sarah. Whatever you need, don't you dare hesitate to ask."

She weakly raises her lips into a grin.

166

"Be careful what you offer me, I may just have to take you up on it, Quinn."

It looks like it will just be the four of us in cabin B-1, which is fantastic. I can handle three women, two of which I know and trust. Crystal may be an enthusiastic fan, but I'm sure she'll get used to sharing a cabin with me and back off of the forced group selfies.

I am without words to describe the feeling of standing in this cabin and getting dressed for welcome dinner, twenty-three years after the last time I did it. After zipping up my shorts and strapping on my bronze gladiator sandals, I take a moment to sit down on the bed and record everything that has happened so far for Jessie. Just like I would do all those years ago, I fold the letter, stick it in an envelope and write "Jess" on the outside with a smiley face. When she'd deliver her letters to me at the end of camp, the envelope would simply say "Q" with a heart underneath. I still have them all, stored away somewhere when I moved to Brigadoon.

Caroline and I try to help Sarah down the stairs on our way to dinner, but she waves us away.

"I'm dying, not helpless," she says as she holds both hands out to show she's perfectly capable of walking on her own. I can't help but smile at her tenacity.

As we arrive at the mess hall, there's a group standing out front and I scan the crowd to see who I recognize. Aiden is by the door speaking to Dave. Pat, who is married, smiles when he sees Sarah. According to her, they've kept in touch and Sarah has joined him and his wife for lunch on a few occasions over the years. I laugh when I see Jake, Jessie's little love interest from those first two summers, and he's balding, pale, and mildly overweight. She eventually let me know the full story of their breakup and it involved Jake getting a little handsy with a girl from Iron River, who promptly told Jessie all about it. She's going to love to hear the news of his unfortunate battle with father time.

I spot Rachel, Trishelle, and a third woman I don't recognize approaching Aiden and cringe. We haven't even hit the age of forty yet and these two appear to have had enough facial injections to kill a horse. I have a sneaking suspicion that they are stay-at-home moms who sell weight loss products online to girls they bullied in high school.

I walk towards Aiden and smile politely at Rachel, Trishelle, and the third woman who now looks familiar, but I can't seem to come up with her name. Rachel and Trishelle look me up and down in disgust. *Oh, here we go.* I can hear my mother whispering *Kill em' with kindness, Quinnie.*

"Rachel, Trishelle! How are you? What have you been up to?"

Trishelle reluctantly speaks to me, only to say that she lives in a gated golf course community with her husband, Chris, who owns an insurance agency in Marquette. I nearly lose my composure when she tells me that she and Rachel have a business together and they've never felt better.

"That's amazing, what kind of business?" I ask.

"Actually, we'd love to tell you about it later. I have some samples back in the cabin," she says with a wink as she hands me her business card. Rachel's facial expression tells me she understands just how much I'm enjoying this and wishes Trishelle would stop talking. I take a quick peek at the card before putting it in my back pocket.

Trishelle Cretens, Independent Distributor, Herbalife.

It takes everything I have not to excuse myself and call Jessie that very moment. I take the card, put it in my back pocket, and smile with more satisfaction than I have in years. My mental celebration is interrupted by Dave, who looks exceedingly proud to be holding a megaphone for the first time in years.

"Attention: campers and staff."

This gets a round of applause, along with a few cheers.

"Thanks to the generosity of Mr. Brooks, we will be dining on cuisine this weekend that's a little nicer than the food you remember from your time at Shady Oaks. No offense, Marge."

"None taken!" Marge yells from inside the mess hall.

"Before we enjoy our delicious meals and reunite with those we haven't seen in years, I'd like to take a second to unveil the statue that will be placed at the entrance to Shady Oaks. Please join me in having a moment of silence for the families of the beautiful souls lost in August of 1999," Dave says as he bows his head.

Aiden walks to the front of the crowd and grips the end of a heavy cream-colored tarp that is placed over the statue. Slight gasps escape the lips of several onlookers when the memorial is unveiled.

The statue is carved out of wood and resembles a mini totem pole. There are several items stacked on top of each other: a basketball, some pom poms, an oversized tube of lipstick, and some football cleats; all carved out of cedar. Whoever made this piece is insanely talented. It's the perfect representation of teenage life, frozen in time. On the bottom of the carved work is a metal plaque with an etched inscription.

Those we have held in our arms for a little while, we will hold in our hearts forever. In loving memory of Vincent Brooks, Jr. and Cassandra Huntington, forever sixteen.

After our moment of silence, I slowly raise my head to see Cassie's parents standing a few feet from the statue, but they aren't looking at it. They are staring directly at me.

Twenty-six

Then

"Bermuda? The Bahamas?" I ask.

"Come on pretty mama. Key Largo, Montego," Aiden continues with a smile. I slap his arm.

"You are so dumb," I smile.

"Well, I'm going to be a microbiologist and you'll be a famous writer, so we can scuba dive wherever you want," Aiden says, squeezing the top of my hand, which is resting on the table between us. We just finished our club sandwiches and Dave is about to make announcements.

It's the Thursday before the end of our two-week session; we all will pack up and go home Saturday for the very last time. The last two weeks have been the best of my life. After my initial hesitation, I really took to scuba diving and have spent the last week dreaming of vacation locales with Aiden where we can practice our skills when we are old enough to travel together.

Despite some micro-aggression on Cassie's part during lessons and an incident where she debatably tried to hold Jessie's head underwater, I think everyone is having a great time.

Things have been a little cold between Jessie and Vinny and I'm not quite sure she believes that he hasn't spent time with Cassie outside of camp. I keep grilling Aiden about it, and he claims not to know anything. I can't tell if he's being honest or just protecting his cousin. I know Vinny really likes Jessie a lot, so I wish he'd just be honest with her or he's going to screw it all up. Because of Jessie's upbringing, she's incredibly independent and will never stick around in a situation longer than she needs to.

"I'd like the following cabins to stay after lunch. If I don't say your cabin number, you are dismissed. B-1, B-2, and A-1, please stick around," Dave announces. A chorus of *Oooooh, they're in trouble* echoes throughout the hall. We roll our eyes, but my curiosity is piqued. What could he want with us? The rest of the nosey campers take their time dumping their trays and exiting the mess hall; they want to know why we're being asked to stay. Dave ushers them out and shuts the double doors behind the last one.

"I know that all of you are a little bummed that the rain this week has ruined your overnight plans," Dave begins. Bummed is putting it mildly. Everyone has been looking forward to theirs – they want something crazy to happen, so they can top our possible encounter with the dogman.

"Well, I got together with your counselors, and we came up with the next best thing. Everyone needs to go pack up their sleeping bags and overnight necessities because we are all going to camp out in the mess hall! Marge and her staff plan to make campfire treats for everyone. It's going to be a great time," he promises.

I'm sure he can read our minds, because he quickly adds, "Because this is a coed sleepover, we will be having extra staff stay the night with you to monitor that the boys are staying on the boys' side and so forth."

He looks around the room at us all.

"Absolutely no funny business."

When the mess hall is cleaned up after dinner tonight, the staff will move all the tables over like they do for the dance, and we are all going to meet at 8pm to start our overnight. Aiden reaches under the table and intertwines his fingers with mine. I cannot believe I'll be sleeping under the same roof as him tonight.

Jessie and I spend entirely too much time trying on pajamas in front of the mirror for our overnight journey to the mess hall.

"How about this outfit? Does it make me look athletic?" I ask, twirling in front of Jessie, who is sitting cross-legged on her bed. I'm wearing a faded B.U.M. Equipment t-shirt and Nike basketball shorts.

"Quinn, you are literally the least athletic human on this earth. Why even try?"

I pick up a pair of folded pajamas from the stack next to her on the bed and lightly slap her with them. She falls backwards on the bed, nearly choking on the Blow Pop she has hanging out of her mouth.

After a few more options, we settle on cute pink pajama pants and a white t-shirt with my white sports bra underneath. I spin in a circle while Jessie spritzes me with a hefty dose of Tommy Girl.

"Lean forward, I read in a magazine that you're supposed to spray your hair. The fragrance will last longer."

Makes sense.

A few more spritzes for good measure and we are on our way to our first coed sleepover. The thought of dad's hypothetical reaction makes my heart drop into my stomach. He wouldn't stop yelling long enough for me to explain the details; I'm sure of it. Some things are just better left unsaid to Jim Harstead.

Aiden and Vinny are outside the front door of the mess hall, laughing about something and wearing matching blue plaid pajamas. Jessie and I look to each other and smile. There's something so attractive about boys our age who are secure enough to laugh at themselves. Vinny sees us smiling as we approach them.

"Hey, our grandmother got us these for Christmas and we'll be damned if we're going to let you two girls make fun of us," he says, hands on his hips.

"Don't make us call our grandma," Aiden says before wrapping his arms around me from behind and taking me in a surprise hold. He leans forward and blows raspberries on my neck, sending me into a fit of laughter.

"No, no, no; this is exactly what I was afraid of," says Dave, stomping towards us. "New rule: don't do anything that your parents would sue me over if they found out about."

"Can you be sued over allowing a lying cheat to stay here?" Cassie says, walking up the path to the mess hall with her girls. She doesn't wait for an answer, only glares at Vinny as she passes.

"I see you've managed to anger Miss Huntington; I'm sure that's been punishment enough, son," Dave speaks in a hushed tone and pats Vinny's back before leaving.

We all smile and pick up our overnight bags, before following Dave into the hall. I chuckle when I see that he has made outlines with masking tape, instructing us where to place our sleeping bags so we don't get too close to someone of the opposite sex. I look back at Jessie and we lay claim on the hot pink taped squares labeled "Girl 4" and "Girl 5," which are not too far from the restrooms.

Sarah, Pat, and Ellen (Marge's niece) stand in the middle of our arranged sleeping bags, which form a semi-circle.

"Ladies and gents, I know it's a bummer that you didn't get to go on a real overnight trip, specifically those of you who are aging out of Shady Oaks. We promise to have as much fun as possible tonight to make it up to you," Pat begins.

Sarah steps forward and takes over, laying out our plans for the night.

"We are going to split off by cabins and spend the next hour coming up with skits to perform for the others. Our judges Jack, Greg, Dave and Marge will determine the winners."

Ellen adds, "The winning team will go home with these priceless trophies."

She turns around and motions for Pat to display the trophies, which are just paper plates that someone has sloppily decorated with "Skit War Champions" in finger paint. This entire plan sounds incredibly dumb, but some of the girls in my cabin seem excited about it and Sarah's enthusiasm is contagious so I suck it up and grab her notebook so we can brainstorm.

Like everything at this camp, what once seemed silly becomes the most fun we've ever had. Our cabin decides to perform a rap about Shady Oaks, and we all dress the part, complete with "gold" chains made from looped paper that we colored with yellow crayons. Everyone in the audience is in tears as we try our best to rhyme and keep our lyrics relevant. We are hardly successful.

Next up is B-2, which includes Cassie, Rachel, Trishelle, and Caroline with their six cabinmates. They do a poetic riff on Shakespeare's "To be or not to be," but change the words to "B-2 or not to B-2," and I'm thrilled to report it's horrible. Poor Caroline knows how bad it is and wisely chooses to stay in the back.

Much to my surprise, the boys of A-1 also do a rap, but their lyrics are about the people of Shady Oaks. We explode with laughter at their perfectly rhymed verses about Marge's pot pies and Pat's "secret crush" on Sarah. They have lines about the Scuba Divas, the dogman, and Dave's hairy legs (which gets a hell of a laugh out of Jessie and me) before finishing their song with lyrics stolen from Hall and Oates about a rich girl and her daddy's money. Nearly every boy looks at Cassie after the last note. She is livid. I only know about Hall and Oates because my mom forced their music on me at an early age. I can't imagine these boys know the lyrics, which means Pat must have helped them. How horrible of a person do you need to be before the counselors are aware of your reputation and help their campers call you out on it?

Cassie performs her usual act when things don't go her way: stomping off to the bathroom to pout. Her two friends attempt to follow her, but Sarah stops them and says she'll handle it. Everyone is buzzing with energy from the skits, and it's so loud in the mess hall, I barely hear the raised voices coming from the bathroom. I edge a little closer to the door to eavesdrop when I hear Sarah say, "Cassie, it was just a joke. You joke all the time. Let's not make a bigger deal of this than we need to."

"Don't try to console me. We both know I don't need to be taking advice from someone with your history," Cassie replies coldly.

The conversation continues too quietly for me to hear, and I quickly bend over, pretending to tie my shoelaces, when Sarah emerges from the restroom moments later. Cassie reenters the room shortly after, a smug smirk on her face.

B-1 ends up winning the competition, but we were nowhere as good as the boys. I'm sure Dave forced his hand on the "judges" not to stir the pot and piss Cassie off further. This is the last year he's forced to deal with a Huntington until 2001, when her younger twin brothers will be old enough to attend. I'm sure he just wants to end the summer on a peaceful note before his next round of spoiled Huntington descendants arrive. We are sure to tell the A-1 boys our theory and assure them they were the better team, to aid in preserving their egos.

Marge has made chocolate pudgy pies for us in the oven as a late-night snack. They are normally cooked over the campfire but taste just as delicious cooked indoors. By the time we finish, we all have gooey brown fingers and chins. There's a constant rotation of campers entering the bathrooms to rinse themselves in a post-sugar daze that results from eating entirely too many pies in one sitting.

I can't imagine the conversation that took place when Dave talked Marge and the janitors into staying overnight with us to chaperone. Although Marge seems overjoyed at the female comradery, the janitors look like they'd rather be anywhere else on earth than keeping thirty teenagers with raging hormones apart for twelve hours. They aren't even wearing pajamas; they are both in some sort of mechanic's jumpsuit as if it's a dirty job they've been assigned to do. I've witnessed them take about seven smoke breaks since we got here. I'm not entirely sure they've been in charge of *any* teenagers before tonight.

"Can we tell ghost stories?" asks one of the girls from B-2. We are all stunned silent; she doesn't know about Jack being Timothy's brother. This was the first year the Timothy skit didn't play out during opening night; I'm sure Dave is doing damage control.

"How about we play a game instead?" Dave suggests.

Jack stands up and we all hold our breath.

"No, Dave, let's tell a ghost story."

We all release those breaths and lower our shoulders when Jack's face morphs into a smile. He doesn't seem to be upset at all. He slowly makes his way to the center of the room, and, for the first time, I notice he walks with a slight limp. Greg, the other janitor, leans forward and turns half the light switches off, leaving the room in an ominous glow from the kitchen bulbs shining through the food line windows. Jack pulls a 5-gallon orange bucket with him and flips it upside down before taking a seat on top. He leans forward and begins his story.

"A part of every childhood is the fun of hearing ghost stories. We all enjoy them. Throughout your life, there's always going to be the one story that stays with 'ya. It chills 'ya to 'yer bones because it disturbs you in a way no other story could. It keeps you up at night, wondering how much to believe and what portion of it was just created by older kids to scare the boots off 'ya. We all have them, but unfortunately mine is from the death of my brother, Timothy."

There is silence from the campers who were here during his admission last year and gasps from those who didn't know.

"Like most good stories told over the years, a lot of what you've heard about Timothy is real and a lot of it isn't. Where do we draw the line between what happened and what is made up? I don't even know the whole story, and I'm his brother."

One hand on his bent knee and the other holding a flashlight with a slightly shaking hand, Jack tells us the story of his last day with Timothy. Shady Oaks held a camp-wide scavenger hunt that went on for hours. Clues were hidden all over the grounds; Jack and his friend Billy even found one in the outhouse. Campers were scattered all over, trying to solve the mystery and be the first to claim the prize at the end. Shortly before mealtime, it was Timothy, his girlfriend Susan, and his friend Frankie who solved the final clue and finished the hunt down at the waterfront. Jack said he'll never forget the pride he felt when his older brother was the star of camp that day. He was the big man on campus.

After dinner, Jack saw his brother talking to some girls outside the mess hall. He patted Jack on the back as he walked by and reminded him to brush his teeth before bed. That would be the last time Jack would ever see his brother.

Just after midnight, the camp was awoken by screams coming from the path to the waterfront. The staff raced down the trail to find Timothy's girlfriend screaming that he had gone under water and hadn't resurfaced. Five or six adults jumped into the water, screaming Timothy's name into the cool, dark night until they didn't have energy left to scream at all.

"Timothy's body wasn't found for days, until divers recovered it. He was tangled in weeds under ten feet of water, which I suppose is why all the folks started telling stories about some sort of monster pulling him under," Jack says, staring at the floor in front of him with wide eyes as if he's only recounting this story to himself, rather than a room full of teenagers.

"What do you think happened?" asks a girl in the back.

"Nobody would believe a ten-year-old kid, but I'm telling you now, I remember everything about the scene like it was yesterday. I saw a small pool of blood on the dock when one of the counselors was shining his light to assist with the search. I didn't say anything at the time, I just turned my head because I knew they were about to find Timothy and I didn't want to see the injury that had caused all that blood. By the next morning, it was cleaned up and they told me I was only imagining things because I was upset."

We are all quietly considering what it would be like for a ten-year-old to experience the death of his only brother in such a horrific manner.

"I started hearing rumblings about Timothy haunting the grounds, and I suppose that is one of the reasons I came back. That's why Greg and I sleep in the abandoned cabins; I offered to fix two of them up in exchange for us living here year-round. Only Greg knew the real reason I wanted to stay there; to see if the rumors were true."

"Well, were they?" asks a boy in the front row.

"I can't tell 'ya for sure, but what I can say is that Greg and I have seen and heard some things in those woods that just don't make sense," Jack answers and Greg, leaning in the kitchen doorway, nods and bows his head slightly.

"I just want you kids to know that I don't mind if you tell ghost stories about the death of my brother, I promise 'ya that. I just want to make sure 'ya include the fact that he was the best big brother I coulda had and he didn't deserve to die that way. I just wish I had some answers about who is responsible for taking Timothy from me."

He wipes a tear from his eye with his weathered index finger, which is curled like a hook. Nobody knows what to say, and luckily, none of us need to, because as soon as he finishes his story, taps begins to play.

Twenty-seven

Now

"They donated the money for that totem pole *and* for the cabin upgrades. I had to invite them to the unveiling."

"I understand that Aiden, but a heads up would have been nice. They aren't my biggest fans," I say, barely above a whisper while we take our seats in the mess hall. Aiden has hired an outside catering company to cook and serve this weekend so Marge and her staff can rest before the real chaos of summer begins. Thankfully, the Huntingtons only stayed long enough to see the memorial plaque and then hopped in their luxury SUV back to Marquette.

"They are gone now, and I'm sorry," he tilts his head in my direction and dimples form as his lips slightly curl. Just like that, I'm sixteen all over again.

"We still have a lot to talk about," I remind him.

"I know, I know. Can we just get through all this mandatory hospitality I need to show and then we can find somewhere quiet and talk about everything that's on your mind?"

I nod. I understand he has obligations.

He quickly stands and clinks a butter knife on his empty glass to get everyone's attention. He welcomes everyone back to camp, acknowledges that it's a bittersweet feeling to reopen after what happened, and talks about his hopes for Shady Oaks in the coming years. He commands an audience like nobody I've ever seen; they are hanging on his every word. When he concludes his speech, he pops open a bottle of champagne and a few drops spill on the tablecloth before he shoves his glass underneath to catch the rest. It is a surreal feeling to see alcohol being poured in the mess hall. The waiters from the catering company open several other bottles and brief cheers sound with every pop of the cork. Within minutes, everyone is conversing and catching up; the resurgence of life on these grounds is a beautiful sight.

"I have something for you," Aiden says as he leans close to my ear.

"Oh really?"

He raises slightly to pull a piece of paper out of his back pocket and hands it to me. It's crumpled and weathered. I slowly unfold it and recognize my own adolescent handwriting. It's the M.A.S.H. game I played with Jessie that very first summer.

"How in the world? I threw this away!"

He beams with pride.

"I know you did, and I also saw how hard you were hiding it from me at the table, so I fished it out of the trash can as soon as you and Jessie walked away."

I stare at the paper with hearts in assorted sizes drawn all around Aiden's name.

"So, you pretty much knew I was obsessed with you the whole time then," I say.

"Oh, yeah. Stage five clinger," he winks, and I throw my head back in laughter.

It's so damn good to have him back.

Twenty-eight

Then

I'm awakened by a hand on my arm in the middle of the night. I'm so confused; I don't know where I am or what time it is, only that it's pitch black. Luckily, as soon as I gain my senses, I can smell that it's him.

"Meet me in the storage room in the back of the kitchen," he whispers.

I'm not alert or sensible enough to argue. I tiptoe over the sleeping bags of my fellow campers, careful not to make a sound. I hold my hands out to feel my way around the kitchen and into the narrow back hall that leads to the dry storage room. The last time I was here, Sarah and I were grabbing sandwiches from Marge after our not-so-successful overnight trip. I'm a little scared, as I can barely see a foot in front of me and have no idea where Aiden is. As I approach what I think is the door to the storage room, a hand reaches out and grabs mine and I gasp. He reaches out his other hand and presses a wrapped stick of gum in my palm.

"Don't be offended, I just know that if it was you that woke me up in the middle of the night, I'd be worried about my breath."

I smile in the dark because it's not very romantic, but he's right. He leads me into the very back of the room, where the shelving units end and there is a bare cedar wall. Neither of us are speaking and I'm worried that he can hear my heart racing or my stomach making noises. I'm not sure if I'm more terrified of what's about to happen or the possibility of getting caught.

I feel his warm hands reach up as he places them around my face and raises it to reach his. His lips touch mine and they are so much softer than I remember. His tongue slowly enters my mouth and I jerk back because I didn't anticipate this, and I have no idea how to kiss like that.

"Relax," he whispers.

I'm not sure what to do with my hands so I just reach them forward and hang my thumbs on the pockets of his pajama pants. We continue to kiss for what may be ten minutes or possibly an hour; I've lost track. It gets easier as we get into a rhythm, and I laugh as his gum somehow transfers to my mouth. He pulls away from my lips, rests his forehead on mine and we both breathe in unison.

"I had to kiss you and it would have been worth it if we got caught."

My thoughts immediately race to my dad getting the call that his daughter was caught sucking face at a coed sleepover. It makes me feel dizzy to consider the repercussions.

"Let's get back before that happens," I whisper. He kisses my forehead and steps back so I can leave first. I make it two steps before he grabs my hand and pulls me back.

"Quinn," he says, his wet lips against my ear.

"Yes?"

"I think I might love you."

Twenty-nine

I am soaring through our final full day of camp. Today I'm looking at Shady Oaks through rose colored glasses; it's where I met my boyfriend *and* my best friend. It will always hold a special place in my heart. I decide I'm going to document everything today: my very last day ever at Camp Shady Oaks.

I begin by snapping a picture of Aiden mid-yawn at breakfast. His hands are outstretched, and his face is wrinkled, yet still adorable.

I snap pictures from a safe distance of Marge and her staff, Greg and Jack, Dave, and the counselors. I want to remember everything.

At lunch, Cassie randomly stops by our table and invites us to a secret meeting after dark tonight. I don't know why she feels that she can speak to us as if we are her friends; she has called Jessie every name in the book since she found out about her relationship with Vinny, and I haven't liked her since the first summer we met.

"What do you mean, secret meeting?" asks Vinny.

Cassie looks around inconspicuously to make sure no adults are within earshot before explaining the details to us.

"The girls and I decided that it's our last night ever at Shady Oaks, so we need to do something crazy. We are only inviting people who we trust to keep this discreet."

"Keep what discreet?" I ask.

"We are going to meet at the waterfront at midnight, when we are sure the counselors are asleep. If the canoes aren't tied up, we are going to take them out to the island and go night swimming."

Jessie snorts.

"And you think our counselors aren't going to wake up when we return in the middle of the night, soaking wet? Count me out."

Cassie turns to the boys.

"Well, it sounds like your girlfriends are chicken, but if you guys are up for the challenge, we'll see you at midnight," she purrs before arching her eyebrows and turning to return to her table.

"Yeah, guys, I just don't know if it would be worth getting caught. It sounds like a lot of risk and who knows how much trouble we'd get in for taking the canoes out without asking," I add after she's gone. I'm shoveling the last of my taco salad in my mouth and not overly concerned with anyone taking Cassie up on her little invitation.

We spend the rest of the afternoon playing tetherball, picking up our finished projects from the arts and crafts building, and using up the rest of our account funds at the canteen. I smile when I see Jack emerge from his cabin in the woods; the same direction I *swore* I saw movement several times that first summer. He smiles and nods when he sees me; everyone who spent last night in the mess hall is now bonded with Jack and that makes me happy. I'm so touched that he trusted us with the story of his brother.

After dinner, we all head down to the waterfront for our last goodbye. Dave has us all wrap our arms over each other's shoulders while we sing acapella, in lieu of the band director playing the trumpet. *Day is done. Gone the sun.* There is something haunting about the sound of a hundred campers singing those words, the empty lake carrying the sound across shores.

Pat has his arm around Sarah's shoulder, and they are both sobbing. She told us that he accepted a position in Boston and will be moving in early September. I know this place has meant just as much to them as it has to us. After the waterfront ceremony, we all walk back up to our cabins in silence. When we get to B-1, I turn to say goodbye to Aiden and he hugs me so tightly, I have to remind him that he'll see me again at breakfast.

Later that night, Jessie is sitting in my bed next to me and we have our legs propped up, reading Cosmopolitan Magazine with our flashlights. We giggle and quickly flip past "101 Tips to Please Your Man in the Bedroom" when Sarah walks by. Jessie goes back to her own bed and clicks her flashlight off. The cabin is now dark, but for the light of the moon through the window by my bed. I drift away into a deep slumber within minutes.

For the second night in a row, I'm jolted awake by a hand on my arm. This time, it's Jessie. I look over at the clock by Sarah's bed. It's 12:01am.

"I think we should go. You only live once, Quinn," she whispers. She has her glasses on, which she wears every night after taking out her contacts.

I groan. I do not want to get out of this comfortable bed, especially not to deal with Cassie Huntington. But again: the promise. I'd do anything for Jess.

I repeat last night's routine of tiptoeing as silently as I can, as to not wake any sleeping campers. I'm very thankful we no longer have the squeaky door when Jessie slowly opens it wide and holds from the top as I crawl under her arm. I sense movement in the cabin and look back; One of the campers (Keri from Ironwood) is lying on her side, facing the door, and watching us. We make direct eye contact and I raise my index finger to my mouth with a shushing motion. She nods in confirmation and closes her eyes. I don't bother telling Jessie.

When we are safely on the path to the waterfront, I slip on my Keds, which are much quieter than flip-flops. Jessie also chose tennis shoes, and we are nearly silent as we cautiously make our way down the edge of the path to the lake. Nearly halfway down to the water, Jessie quickly puts her arm straight out to her side, blocking me from moving any further. She brings her finger in front of her lips and gives me the same signal I gave Keri moments earlier. I stay silent. I turn my head towards the lake when I detect motion, but it isn't Cassie, her friends, or our boyfriends. It's Jack.

He is sitting on a stump that he has pulled to the edge of the water and his feet are ankle-deep in the lake. He is staring at the moon, and I can see his shoulders heaving slightly. He is crying. Jessie and I watch him for a moment, before he stands up, returns the stump back with the rest of the wooden log benches, and bends down to towel his feet dry. Jessie and I slowly retreat to the edge of the woods, and crouch down behind a large fallen tree. Jack puts his shoes back on, slings the towel over his shoulder, and walks up the path, head down. He doesn't notice us. We wait another five minutes before we are brave enough to come out of the woods and finish our trek down to the lake.

I don't see Aiden, Vinny, Cassie, or her friends. Maybe they saw Jack and it spooked them. Maybe they already left for the island.

"Look," Jessie says, pointing towards the canoe racks. There are several missing, along with a pile of shoes. "They already left."

I take my disposable camera out of my sweatshirt pocket and snap a shot of the pile of shoes. Then I take a picture of the full moon over the lake. I want to remember my surroundings during the most rebellious night of my existence.

"Well, if we're going to do it, let's do it."

I shrug.

We carefully flip a canoe over, push it to the edge of the water, toss the paddles in the boat and Jessie holds it while I climb in. The minute we push off, I can see flashlights out on the island, which is located just a couple hundred yards from the shore. My first instinct is to scold them when we get there; any adult could easily see those lights and it would get us all caught.

We glide seamlessly in the water towards the bouncing lights on the island. The lake is calm as it's ever been as we float forward. I still cannot believe we are doing this.

Once we are close enough to make out the shapes of bodies on the sand, we give one last push with our paddles and let the momentum carry us to the shore. I reach my paddle forward to stop us when we hit land, and that's when I see two figures, up against a tree kissing. I guess we now know the real motive behind this midnight meeting.

"Cassie, what the fuck?" I hear a voice snap. It sounds like Vinny. As I get one leg out of the boat, I realize it *is* Vinny. I'm shocked to see several half-empty bottles of alcohol in the sand next to five or six other campers, who have their toes in the water. There are also two or three people wading in deeper water, each with plastic cups in their hands. I had no idea there would be so many campers invited, and I definitely didn't know anything about alcohol being involved. I would have never come; it's just not worth being caught.

I turn my attention towards Vinny and his line of sight, and I wonder if the dark could be affecting my vision this much, because I can't believe what I'm seeing.

Cassie is pulling away from the other figure I saw in the shadows; the other half of the kiss I witnessed when I was pulling up to the beach. She giggles and wipes her mouth, grabbing a bottle out of the sand as she makes her way to her friends in the water. I look to the tree they were leaned against and squint to confirm what I'm seeing.

It's Aiden.

Thirty

"Quinn, no wait, it's not what you think!"

It's even more insulting that he's chosen to shout the most overused words in the history of infidelity. I don't stick around to let him *try* and explain himself. I put my foot right back in the canoe and push us off. We're going back. I hear Aiden scrambling to get in a canoe and follow us; it only makes me paddle faster. I never want to see him again.

"It's going to be okay. Everything is going to be okay," Jessie keeps repeating as we get closer to camp. "Just breathe."

I somehow make it back to shore and jump out of the canoe. I grab my shoes from the pile next to the canoe racks and hastily put them on. As soon as I walk to leave, I hear a crunch. Jessie's glasses.

"I took them off so nobody would see me with them. It's no big deal, I have plenty of contact lenses," she is rapidly speaking, sensing that I'm on the edge of hysteria and breaking my best friend's glasses might just be the final push.

"I'm so sorry," I say slowly. I'm in a daze. I cannot believe what has happened to my perfect life in the last ten minutes.

She slips her shoes on, pulls the canoe a little further up on the sand and abandons it so she can wrap her arm around me and guide me up the incline towards the path back to the cabin. I'm shaking from the cold and from the shock. I just didn't think he was capable of this. He isn't like the other guys our age. He's different. When we make it past the log benches and to the path, I collapse. My knees just give out. I'm on the ground sobbing as quietly as I can.

I hear the sound of another boat hitting the shore and footsteps rapidly approaching us. Aiden drops to his knees beside me and puts his hand on my back, but I shrug it away.

"Quinn, you have to listen to me, please," he whispers.

"She doesn't have to do shit, Aiden," Jessie aggressively barks back in a hushed tone.

He ignores her.

"She told us you were coming, so we snuck out just before midnight to meet you guys. When we got to the waterfront, she told us you both had just taken a canoe to the island, so we went to follow you."

I slowly lift my head to meet his gaze. I have to know how much of this is a lie and his eyes will tell me everything I need.

"Cassie and her friends stole alcohol from the counselor's lounge. Vinny and I immediately wanted to leave; neither of us can afford to get in trouble. We both just made Varsity."

Ah, great. He's making this about him when he just broke my fucking heart.

"We told her we were leaving and how I was pissed because she lied about you guys being there. That's when we saw your canoe coming. We were so relieved and were headed towards the shore to meet you. When you got within a few feet of us, Cassie pushed me up against a tree and kissed me. Vinny yelled and I panicked and froze. You have to believe me, Quinnie."

Cassie's lips were on Aiden's. I don't think I'll ever be okay.

"You don't get to call me that anymore," I whisper, without emotion.

Jessie pulls me back up to my feet and I reach down to dust my knees off. We walk slowly back to the cabin, and I turn once to look at Aiden. He is still on his knees, in the dirt, eyes closed.

A few hours later, there is a bird chirping right outside my window. I lift my head and look around; everyone is still sleeping. Reveille hasn't played yet, so I must have some time left.

I sense movement and reopen my eyes. It's Pat. In the girl's cabin, where he most definitely does not belong. He is kneeled next to Sarah's bunk, speaking in a panicked but hushed tone. I hear the last few words of his sentence: *didn't come back last night.*

Is he talking about Aiden?

Sarah throws a pair of sweatpants on and pulls a Camp Shady Oaks hoodie over her head before throwing on her Adidas slides. She looks around the cabin, so I quickly shut my eyes.

Reveille never plays, but the commotion outside is enough to wake the rest of the girls. We groggily stumble out of the cabin, toothbrushes in hand, on our way to the latrine. The voices we hear are coming from the waterfront and we all stop in our tracks to listen.

It's Lena who emerges on the path first, running towards us.

"Get back in your cabins, everyone. Stay there until further notice," she commands, her voice shaking.

Thirty-one

Now

I return from dinner a little buzzed from the champagne and the relief of a successful first night. I sit on my bed and write a letter to Jessie about everything that happened tonight.

Caroline is Facetiming her kids before bed and Crystal is typing up an entry for her blog. Sarah is sitting on her bed, looking around the room with a slight grin on her face. I'm sure she can't believe how much this place has changed and somehow stayed the same. I tiptoe over to her, and she pats the bed for me to sit down.

"I'm so proud of you, Quinn. I'm sorry I haven't reached out about your success, but please know how proud I am of you."

I rub her back with my right hand and we both stare out the window at the full moon.

"I know it's tough to be back here, but I'm so glad you came," I tell her.

She sighs.

"Some horrible decisions were made the last time we were here. Decisions that ruined lives and destroyed a place that caused so much joy for so many years," she says, still staring out the window.

We all share blame in what happened that night. I should have never left the cabin. None of us should have. I nod in agreement but don't speak. She slowly lies down in her bed, and I pull the comforter up over her shoulders. She closes her eyes and I keep my hand on her back, lightly rubbing it until she falls asleep.

The next morning, I wake up early and leave the cabin in search of coffee. Surely, we have other early risers here who have put on a pot. I can't wait to enjoy a steaming hot mug without Christy berating me over my caffeine intake. When I open the screen door, I'm startled to see Aiden walking towards me with two Styrofoam cups in his hand.

"Good morning," he says with a smile, handing me one of the cups.

"A good morning, indeed," I reply.

We walk down to the waterfront together and I remember just how beautiful this lake is in the morning. I hear a familiar eerie cry and smile as I see a pair of loons in the water. They often wake me at Brigadoon, but I've grown to love the sound. There is an elderly couple in kayaks, gliding along the calm waters. Aiden motions for me to sit next to him on a freshly built bench, a world of improvement over the sawed-off logs that gave us all splinters the last time I sat here.

"So, let's talk," he says. "What do you want to know?"

That's a loaded question.

"Well, I suppose the top question my therapist would like an answer to is: why did you abandon me after what happened?"

He laughs. "Ouch."

I'm staring at the ground in front of us as he continues to speak. There is a trail of ants traveling a few inches from my feet. I take a sip of the coffee he brought me. It might just be the best coffee I've ever had.

"In hindsight, I'd obviously do a lot of things differently. But I was also sixteen. I had just lost my cousin, who was also my best friend. My parents were grieving and whisked me and my sister back to Florida immediately. I was being questioned by lawyers and they warned me that anything I said to others could be used against me if I were charged. I was scared to death, Quinn."

I laugh, with a hint of condescension.

"We were all scared, Aiden. I'm sorry you lost Vinny, but I was dealing with the detectives as well."

"I guess I just wanted to put the whole ordeal behind me, so when you wrote the book, it was hard to understand your motives. I didn't know why you'd want to bring up an event that we wanted so badly to move on from."

He's got a point. Writing is an escape for me and revisiting the most tragic experience of my life was somehow cathartic. My only mistake was not considering how it would affect the other people involved that night. I even donated some of the proceeds to a charity that Cassie's parents set up, but they returned the check.

"Because she's a greedy, selfish bitch," bellows a scratchy, masculine voice. We both turn to see who is behind us. Although he's now in his seventies, I recognize the janitor from all those years ago.

"Greg?" I ask in disbelief. He wasn't at last night's dinner; I'm sure of it. Immediately after I say his name, a lightbulb goes off.

"Wait, *greedy, selfish bitch?* That's the name that was repeated over and over in the threatening letters and emails I received. *It was you?*"

Aiden stands quickly, his fists balled with fury.

"You're the one that threatened Quinn's life? For what, Greg? For what?"

He looks around, as if he's too angry to even look me in the eyes. He spits aggressively in the ground next to him before speaking.

"Do you know what you did to Jack's legacy? Millions of people read that book and then watched the damn thing play out on cable. That's millions of people who questioned whether Jack was capable of harming those poor kids."

I set my coffee down and put both hands up, showing I'm harmless as I walk a little closer to him. He's shaking.

"Greg, I wrote a factual book about the events of August of 1999. Part of being a responsible writer is to tell things from all angles. I did a chapter on each person who was ever a suspect in the murders, myself included on that list. I had to mention Jack, he was seen at the scene of the crime."

"Yeah, by you and your crazy bitch friend," he shouts.

"Okay, that's enough," yells Aiden, taking large strides toward Greg. He pulls his iPhone out of his pocket and hits a few buttons, before speaking into the receiver. "Yep, by the waterfront. Male in his seventies, gray hair, navy t-shirt and dark jeans."

Greg is still spouting hateful comments at me when two police officers jog down the path and apprehend him, leading him away with a zip tie around his wrists.

"I knew there was a good possibility of *someone* acting crazy this weekend, so I have guards stationed at the gate. I just never imagined it'd be Greg."

I stare at the spot he was just standing, his spit still wet in the dirt. He has had so much anger towards me for so many years. I cannot believe he was the person behind the threats I received. Everything about my life changed because of those letters. They put me in such a dark mental state for so many years.

"Ironically, I brought you down here to show you another plaque I had installed," Aiden says, bringing me over to the edge of the woods.

Right near the waterfront, there is a bronze statue of a grown man and a little boy sitting on a dock, feet dangling over the edge. The inscription reads:

In loving memory of the Myers Brothers
Timothy Myers 1942-1958
Jack Myers 1948-1999

"It's beautiful," I say.

Aiden and I sit back on the bench, finish our coffees, and tell each other everything we've been wanting to say for the last twenty years. I think we've both harbored resentment towards each other over things that were out of our control and largely based on misunderstandings. Today feels like a fresh start.

He walks me back up to my cabin so I can get showered and ready for lunch, which will be another deliciously catered meal. My mouth is watering just thinking of it. I can hear voices in B-1 as we near the porch.

"I really wish you'd stop," a voice yells, and I'm sure it's Sarah.

I look to Aiden with confusion, and we both hurry through the screen door to investigate.

Sarah is standing next to my bed with folded arms while two women are going through my suitcase. It's Trishelle and Rachel. Rachel has my stack of letters addressed to Jessie in her hand. They spin around to face us when we enter the cabin.

"What the hell are you doing?" I ask.

She holds the envelopes in the air.

"No, what the hell are *you* doing and why are you keeping in touch with a murderer?"

Thirty-two

"She's not a murderer!" I yell, my emotions taking over.

"Oh, really? Her broken glasses were found two feet from the crime scene, Quinn. How does your little friend explain that?"

"Jessie would never hurt Vinny, she loved him!" I scream.

"Aiden, she is crazy. Like off-the-wall, batshit, legitimately crazy. I can't believe you invited her here!" shouts Rachel, pointing in my direction.

"What are you talking about?" Aiden asks, his hand still on my back from when we entered the cabin.

"Where do you think she has been for the last couple years? She's been locked up in a high-end loony bin. Oh, and the kicker? It's on Lake Timothy! She's probably been watching you! I bet they are hunting her down right now for escaping!"

I shake my head. This is not how I wanted him to find out. I was going to tell him where I live, I swear.

"My uncle went there to repair the internet lines after she had a mental breakdown and cut them all. He said it's some off-the-radar mental health facility in the middle of the woods and Quinn's been on full lockdown by an armed staff," Trishelle adds, aggressively nodding her head as she continues. "Oh, and remember how she told us all her mom left the family? That was a lie, too. She was dead! This whole time. Dead. She lied to us all for years."

"Is that true?" Aiden asks, slowly dropping his hand from my back. I don't know where to begin. Rachel doesn't even give me time to start.

"Does anyone think maybe *she* is the one who killed Cass and Vinny? Or maybe she helped Jessie? She worked so hard to cast the suspicion on everyone around her when she wrote her little book. Now we know she's a pathological liar. We need to tell the police."

"That's enough!" Sarah screams and everyone goes silent.

The dizziness takes over and I grab onto the nearest bed post to steady myself. Without thought, I reach down and grab my bag, stuffing the few loose items I have into it. I also grab my closed suitcase before running out of the cabin without turning around to see the scene play out in my wake.

I sprint until I get to my vehicle. I don't have the keys. I hung them on a hook in the fancy new locker by my bed. I don't care. I drop my suitcase next to my car and run.

I run down the gravel drive to the welcome sign for Shady Oaks. I take a right and run until I hit the trail home. I run without emotion. I keep going through the woods until I reach the back door of Brigadoon. I reach under a rock, retrieve the spare key, and let myself inside. I somehow manage to disarm the alarm with my shaking hands. The light turns green, the system beeps, and I collapse on the floor.

Thirty-three

Then

It didn't take long for the news to spread: two bodies have been found in Lake Timothy. I sit in my bed and sob, thinking of Aiden. I am disgusted with myself for not believing his story. Jessie wraps her arms around me while I cry. Neither of us say a word.

Within an hour, the entire grounds of Shady Oaks are swarming with police officers, most of them wide-eyed and overwhelmed. These are probably the first suspicious deaths that most of them have encountered in their careers. Things like this just don't happen in the Upper Peninsula of Michigan.

Dave knocks on the door to our cabin and enters without waiting for a response. Sarah has been in and out; speaking with Pat and the other counselors but is now sitting on her bed with a pillow in her lap, hugging it tightly.

"Ladies, please gather round so I can speak with you," Dave says with a solemn tone. "This is never an easy conversation to have, but two of your fellow campers lost their lives last night. It appears that Vincent Brooks and Cassandra Huntington drowned in the lake."

Sobs ring out across the cabin. It's not that these girls knew Vinny very well or particularly liked Cassie, but two sixteen-year-olds lost their lives. I turn to Jessie, and she is shaking her head.

"No," she says.

"Miss Broeders, I'm sorry to say, but yes, their identities were confirmed moments ago. That's why I'm here."

I hug Jessie tightly, but she doesn't move. She's sitting straight up on my bed, arms to her side, staring forward. I look over her shoulder as I'm hugging her and stare blankly at the wall. This can't be real.

"All of your parents have been called and they are on their way to pick you up. I need everyone to finish packing up your belongings and stay in the cabin until a parent arrives to bring you home," Dave says. "Jessie, we haven't been able to get ahold of your parents yet, but we'll keep trying."

"She can come home with me," I say.

My dad is the first parent to burst through the door, hours before he was scheduled to arrive for our normal Saturday departure. I've only seen him cry once in my life, but his face is red and tear-soaked when he scoops me up in his arms and hugs me so tightly, I can't breathe.

"Get your things," he says sternly. "Jessie, you, too."

"Dave said he's going to try and call my parents again," Jessie says, hopeful.

"Jessie baby, I talked to your dad. You're going to come stay with us for a couple days."

She understands everything that wasn't said and grabs her faded pink bag, careful to hold the top together where the zipper has torn apart.

When we leave the cabin, there is a police officer outside the door.

"Hello, sir," he says to my father. "I just need the girls' names and contact information so we can reach out for a statement."

I can tell dad wants to argue. He wants to tell the man we've been traumatized enough by the death of our friends. He instead chooses the peaceful option of simply reaching in his wallet to retrieve one of his business cards.

"That's our home address and phone number. My daughter is Quinn, and her friend is Jessie Broeders. She'll be staying with us for a few days so it may be best to just contact me in regard to both girls."

The officer nods and dad takes both our bags before ushering us up the path towards his Silverado. He throws them in the bed of the truck and, as we are about to load into the cab, an officer shouts for us to stop.

"Sorry, excuse me. I just have one question before you go. Do these look familiar to either of you?"

He produces a small, sealed plastic bag marked evidence. He lifts it with his gloved hand in front of both of us to inspect.

"Yes, those are my glasses. Quinn accidentally stepped on them last night and I forgot to pick them up," Jessie says.

The officer stares at her just a moment too long for my comfort. He's wondering if she's lying; I'm sure of it.

"You're good to go, Mr. Harstead. We'll be in touch."

Thirty-four

We already thought our lives had been turned upside down, but they free fall when the autopsy reports are released.

Vinny died from of blunt force trauma and was dead shortly after being submerged in water, and Cassie's cause of death was listed as drowning. Cassie had alcohol in her system; Vinny did not. No illegal drugs were detected for either victim, but Cassie's results showed prescription meds for anxiety. There is no end to the scenarios that are discussed, both by the detectives on the case and by the public.

Were they star-crossed lovers? Did he slip and fall? Did she kill him by accident and then let herself sink under the waters of Lake Timothy because she couldn't live without him?

Did any of us other campers have something to do with it? Jessie and I both had motives, according to the detectives. She had been trying to steal Jessie's boyfriend all summer and had just been caught sucking face with mine. Could Jessie have broken her glasses while fighting with the victims?

Was it a random killer, on the hunt for teenagers? What about all those paranormal stories – did Timothy do this?

Rumors were especially rampant of Aiden being the culprit; people were saying he was in love with Cassie and killed them both after catching them together. That one hurt to hear.

The moment that changed everything happened when they went to question Jack for a second time, less than a week after the murders and found that he had hung himself, right there in the renovated, formerly abandoned cabin at the edge of the property. He tied a belt to the wooden beam at the center of the room and left no note. Everyone had the same thought: *It must be an admission of guilt. That monster killed those children.*

Jessie and I repeatedly told the investigators that it was before we even went to the island when we saw Jack sitting at the lake. He wasn't in a violent rage; he was somber and appeared to be mourning his brother. We saw him leave, heading towards his cabin on the other side of the property. They didn't want to listen. They only wanted us on record, saying we saw Jack at the scene of the crime, and nothing else. Case closed.

Well, it would have been case closed, if they had any evidence. Their strongest theory was that Jack was still upset over the bathroom encounter with Cassie, years earlier. Jack received no reprimand from the camp over this incident; yet people felt he was still angry enough to hold her under water until she stopped breathing. There was no DNA tying him to the crime, nor a single shred of legitimate evidence, other than the fact that we saw him at the lake hours before the murders.

Because they couldn't prove without a doubt that Jack was responsible for the murders, the case remained open.

Thirty-five

Now

"Deep breaths, Quinn. Deep breaths."

Christy got a security alert on her phone and saw that I was home early and distraught so, being the angel that she is, left her visit with her mother and sped home to console me.

"Is that really what people think of me?" I cry out, my face buried in the sleeve of her sweater. She smells like fabric softener and butterscotch candy.

"No, Quinn. You let two miserable bitches get the best of you. They have nothing better to do than try to make others as unhappy as they are."

"I was just a kid when mom died. I didn't know how to process the grief, so I just pretended she moved away. It was so much easier that way. If only I had seen a therapist twenty-five years ago."

I wipe the tears from my cheeks and lean back up against the kitchen wall, where I'm still seated from my arrival back home an hour earlier.

"Do you think I'm crazy? I can't believe they think I'm capable of actually killing someone."

Christy huffs and gets on her feet. She grabs me by both elbows and pulls me up from the floor.

"Quinn Harstead, we have known each other too long for this bullshit. You're in therapy now because it's the right thing to do after all you've been through. Anyone that has taken two minutes to get to know you knows damn well you wouldn't hurt a fly. Now, put the words from those ugly human beings out of your head and let's move on."

"I also just can't believe it was Greg all these years. It was Greg who I was so afraid of."

"Well, you don't have to be afraid anymore."

I give her a weary smile.

"Can I take one drug-induced nap and I promise I'll never ask again? I just need to sleep this off and start over."

She smiles back.

"Just this once, Quinn. Just this once."

When I wake, the house is silent. I can tell by the position of the sun that it's late afternoon. I'm not sure I've ever been so thirsty in my life. I walk down the stairs to grab a water from the fridge and see by the clock on the stove that I was asleep for hours. Just what I needed. I'm a little groggy from the sleeping pills, but I'll shake it off. I always do.

Christy has left a note on the counter, *Be right back,* and my heart sinks. I know exactly where she went. Damn it, Christy.

216

I left my shoes by the back patio door, so I throw them on and repeat my actions from this morning: I sprint through the woods, to the road, and down the gravel drive to Camp Shady Oaks. I see Christy's SUV parked haphazardly outside the mess hall, like she arrived in a hurry. Or a fit of rage.

I want to warn Aiden, but he never even told me what cabin he was staying in, nor do I know where he'd be this time of day. I don't have to look far, as I hear his voice coming from an open window in the mess hall. I crouch down and sit below the window to eavesdrop. I'm not ready to announce my return just yet.

"Okay, now that I've got you all here, I'd like to give the floor to Christy. She came here to set some things straight about Quinn and I'd appreciate it if you'd let her finish before opening your mouths."

I've never heard Aiden speak with such authority. I kind of like it. I hold my breath as I hear Christy begin to speak.

"You ladies are going to listen to me, particularly you two in the front who apparently had a whole lot to say this morning."

I hear Rachel begin to object and Aiden shushes her. I'm living for this.

"Yes, when Quinn was barely fourteen years old, her mother died unexpectedly. It nearly broke her. She didn't feel like talking about it at summer camp. She doesn't owe you an explanation for that, I assure you."

She pauses to make sure nobody is going to argue her point. Wisely, they don't.

"Quinn suffered a loss here at camp, just like all of you. Her own best friend was briefly questioned for the murders and is still considered a suspect in a lot of your minds. Quinn wrote a book because it was like therapy for her, and her life was threatened as a result. Repeatedly. She lost any sense of security she had. She went from a best-selling author to a recluse who is afraid to sit in her own back yard, because she'd be too exposed."

I hear another pause and I know it's because Christy is getting emotional. She really does love me.

"You want to start a rumor that her home is some sort of mental hospital? Let me tell you about her home, which is named Brigadoon, by the way. That home is a safe haven for her. It is a fortress, in the middle of the woods, that she spent more money on than you could imagine so she wouldn't be up all night wondering who was coming to carry out the threats she was receiving."

I hear her heels clicking across the wooden floors, and I soon know exactly who she's standing in front of.

"And us *staff* who stay at the house? Well, first, there's me. I had just gone through a bad divorce; my abusive ex ruined my credit and my self-esteem. Quinn gave me a job, making more than I have in my life and she treats me like family. Randall, her cook? His parents died and so did his dreams of going to culinary school. Quinn heard about it and paid for his tuition. She also lets him live in the guest house for free and pays him a whole lot of money to cook her dinner. Bruce, who runs security, is a Vietnam veteran who suffers from PTSD and anxiety, which makes it hard for him to work with others. Again, Quinn heard about his story and gave him a job with full benefits where he can sit in a room and monitor the security cameras all day. This girl you've made out to be a monster has saved more lives than you'll ever know. So, I strongly suggest you keep her name out of your little mouths."

I want to stand and clap. I've never had someone stick up for me like Christy is.

"Does anyone have any further questions?" Aiden asks, but I've heard enough. I crawl past the windows and to the front of the mess hall, where I jog down the path to quickly grab my car keys from B-1.

On the way back, I stand with my back against the building to hear if they are still inside.

"And that's why nobody liked either of you back then, and they still don't like you now. You're both miserable little shits."

It's Sarah. She's letting Rachel and Trishelle have it.

I walk quietly to my car with a smile before driving back home to Brigadoon.

Thirty-six

"I can't thank you enough for staying so long. I guess I just had a lot to talk about today," I say to Vicki, my therapist, as she's grabbing her keys to go.

"Quinn, I'm happy to help. I feel like you've had a breakthrough and I couldn't be happier. I'm looking forward to hearing how you feel a month from now."

I hesitate for a moment with my hand on the front doorknob before I open it.

"So, Christy heard from one of her friends at the jail in Escanaba that you're testifying at Heather Matthews' trial. Any chance you want to talk to me about it?"

Vicki smiles and shakes her head.

"Not a chance in hell. But good luck with that book," she says with a wink.

"Who says I'm writing a book about it? I'm retired."

"Yeah, Quinn, and I'm the Queen of England."

I swing the front door open for her to leave and see a black Range Rover pulling up in front of my garage. I lean back into Bruce's office, and he just shrugs and smiles.

"Some kind of security," I say. "Bye Vicki, I'll see you next month."

As she is walking to get into her sedan, Aiden exits the Range Rover with papers in his hand and heads towards me. Vicki does a quick spin behind his back and raises her eyebrows a few times, giving me a thumbs up before opening her car door.

It's been over a week since I left Shady Oaks and I've been admittedly avoiding his calls and texts. I just need time to process everything that happened and allow him space to get his camp open for the season.

I furrow my brows and stand with my arms crossed as he approaches me.

"We need to talk," is all he says before pushing past me, into the house, like he's been here before.

He looks to his left and right before noticing Bruce's office, where he leans in and produces an envelope from his back pocket. He hands it to Bruce while shaking his hand.

"Nice to finally meet you in person, Bruce. Here are those Packers tickets I promised. Twenty-yard line, about nine rows up. You are going to love the seats."

Bruce looks like a kid on Christmas.

"Are you kidding me? You bribed my security to let you in the gates?"

"Miss Harstead, my job is to protect you from any threats and, as far as I can tell, Mr. Brooks is no threat to your well-being."

I laugh and shake my head. *What else can I do?*

"Where can we talk?" Aiden asks. He's not smiling.

"My office is right down the hall," I say, pointing in its direction. "Can I get you something to drink?"

"No, I'm good," he responds.

"Good, Christy's off today, and I don't know where we keep anything," I joke.

He doesn't laugh.

"Wow, okay. Let's go have that talk."

We sit down next to each other on the velvet couch in my office, which doesn't get used much. I swear, I get writing done anywhere in this house *except* the office. My last novel was written almost entirely from my bed. I should bring that up when pretentious interviewers ask me to describe my *process*. My process is pajamas, Pringles, and a prayer, lady.

Aiden puts his hand on my thigh, and it sends electricity through my body; I wasn't expecting it. He sets his paperwork on his lap and grabs my hand, looking into my eyes.

"What's so urgent?" I ask.

"Quinn, Sarah passed away a few days ago."

No.

I just saw her. Sure, she looked sick, but she was mobile. She was feisty. She still looked like she had so much life left.

"That isn't all."

"What?"

"My aunt and uncle, Vinny's parents, just received a letter in the mail."

Aiden grabs an envelope from his stack and opens it, pulling out one sheet of paper, which he hands to me. I unfold it to reveal beautiful pink stationary with white doves scattered on the top. The font reminds me of my mom's old typewriter. My hands begin to shake when I scan to the end and see Sarah's name before I begin reading the letter.

To the families of Vinny Brooks and Cassie Huntington,

If you are reading this letter, it means I went out a coward. I died without having the guts to tell you the truth. I am so sorry you have to find out this way.

On that late August night in 1999, I woke up in the middle of the night to the sounds of one of my campers crying in her bed. When I sat up, the noises stopped, so I knew whoever it was didn't want to talk to me about it. Since I was up anyway, I took a trip to the latrine. While I was on my way there, I heard some sort of argument coming from down by the lake.

I followed the voices, which led me to the waterfront. Cassie and Vinny were at the end of the dock in a heated argument. I couldn't hear everything that was said, but Vinny seemed to be upset with Cassie over "ruining" something and kept telling her to apologize. What I did hear clearly is Vinny telling Cassie that she's a miserable liar, and he pushed past her to walk down the dock towards the shore. It all happened so fast. She reached over to grab an oar and swung at him from behind. Vinny wasn't expecting it and wasn't able to brace himself for the impact.

I sprinted down the dock and jumped into the water to help him, but I was too late. Just as the autopsy confirmed, he died on impact. I couldn't believe it.

I looked up at Cassie and, I swear on everything holy, she smiled. I know that's hard for her family to hear, but it's the truth. In that moment, I lost my mind. I lost any good sense I had in my body. I pulled myself up on the dock, charged at Cassie and she fell backwards, pulling both of us into the water on the other side of the dock. I can't explain the feeling of blind rage, but I felt it that night as I pushed Cassie under water while she struggled. Everything I'd seen Cassie do and say over the years flashed through my mind as I held her head under that cold, dark water. Mr. and Mrs. Huntington, I killed your daughter.

I can't even explain what happened next because I only remember flashes of it. I must have showered at some point. I must have put on dry clothes. My next memory is being wakened by Pat, to tell me one of his campers was missing.

I know that the entire town suspected the other kids at first. Then, their suspicion turned to Jack when he took his own life shortly after. Everyone assumed that it was because of his guilty conscience, and I let them believe it. In reality, Jack was a tortured soul who suffered from depression after losing his entire family. I think the deaths of Cassie and Vinny just freshened the hurt of what happened to his brother, and he couldn't take it. I should never be forgiven for any of my acts, but especially not for allowing this world to think Jack Myers was capable of violence.

I'm sorry I didn't have the guts to tell you this while I was still around. May this life give you the happiness you deserve and the strength to heal.

Sarah Lewis

Thirty-seven

One year later

"Quinn Harstead, you're going to be late!" Christy shouts up the stairwell.

I appear at the top of the stairs and do a twirl. I'm wearing a brand-new black dress and shoes that I was entirely too excited about finding on clearance. Christy is standing at the bottom with her arms crossed and a reluctant smile on her face.

"You might want to say that again," Aiden says, clearing his throat and appearing next to her in his suit and tie. Dear lord, he's handsome.

"You're right. I've just been yelling the same name for so many years. Let's try this again," she pretends to cough a few times before yelling, "Mrs. Quinn Brooks, wife of the incomparable Aiden Brooks, you're going to be late!"

Aiden wraps her in a head lock, and she squeals with laughter.

"Are you sure you don't want to come with us?" he asks her as I carefully navigate the stairs in my heels.

"Believe it or not, I have a date," she says, before turning away, not offering us anymore information. Aiden and I can't hide our shock. I've never seen Christy go on a date. I haven't heard her so much as mention another man since her divorce. When I get to the bottom of the stairs, the front door swings open and Bruce walks in, carrying a bouquet of spring flowers. Christy hastily grabs her coat and hurries him out the door before we can even say hello. I'm sure she can hear us hollering and clapping from outside the door. Christy and Bruce? I would have never seen it coming, but I wholeheartedly approve.

"Ready for the ball, Mrs. Brooks?"

I can't believe Shady Oaks has been open for a full year. The first season was so successful, applications doubled for this year. We are doing a fundraiser tonight and have invited anyone we know with deep pockets and several that we don't. The goal is to raise enough money that no family will ever be turned away from Shady Oaks due to lack of funds. We are calling it the Jack Myers Memorial Fund. We even invited Greg, with whom I've made amends and refused to press charges against. To our surprise, we received a rather hefty donation from Mr. and Mrs. Huntington, and the letter was addressed to both Aiden *and* me. I think Sarah's confession gave them the closure they needed to stop hating all the wrong people. I heard they even called to apologize to the detective that they'd been harassing for years after Sarah's admission was made public and the case was officially closed.

I check myself in the hallway mirror before grabbing my coat. Aiden appears in the reflection behind me, wrapping his arms around my waist.

"You don't need to check; I can verify that you're still stunning."

I turn to kiss him, and we're interrupted by the front door swinging open again, but this time it's Jessie. She's all dolled up in a blue satin dress and looks like a million bucks.

"Guys, quit playing grab ass, I've been waiting in your Jeep for twenty minutes! We're going to be late!"

Jessie began working for me three months ago; she does all my tour and speaking engagement scheduling and handles my public relations. She has a way with words and is doing a fantastic job. I even gave her my old office at Brigadoon, after admitting that I never actually get any writing done in there. It's nice having her around.

I turn to grab my coat from the rack by the door. Directly next to it is a framed piece of paper, its edges still crumpled from all those years ago. That fateful game of M.A.S.H., which boldly predicted I'd live in a mansion in the middle of the woods with Aiden, no kids, and a brand-new Jeep. I guess it wasn't such a silly game after all.

"Did you bring a signed copy of your new book for the auction?" Aiden asks as I pull my coat on.

"Damn it, I forgot. I'll just grab an extra copy from Jessie's office and sign it quick."

He gives me a dramatic eye roll, like it's not usually him making us late for every function we attend.

I run down the hall to her office, flip on the light, and spot her shelf with all the extra copies of my books. I take a moment to admire all the titles; who would have thought I could make a career out of this? I don't stop and appreciate how far I've come nearly enough. I scan my fingers across the freshly printed spines of my newest release, *Murder and Revenge in Delta County*, before pulling a copy down to sign. My moment of self-appreciation is interrupted by a quick beep of the horn outside; I'm not sure if it's Jessie or Aiden, but I know they are both losing patience.

I scan her desk for a Sharpie or anything I can use to scribble my name and get out of here. I pull open several of her drawers with no luck. She has a laptop bag under the desk, so I reach forward and unzip it. I pull it towards me, into the light, to search the bottom of her bag, which is a total mess. I think I feel a pen, so I remove her MacBook and a few other items and set them next to me while I retrieve it.

As I'm grabbing the stack of items to put back in her bag, a notepad slips out from behind her laptop. I bend to pick it up and my heart stops.

It's pink, and before I even flip it over, I somehow know.

I hold it in my shaking hands briefly before dropping it to the ground, where it lands face down, concealing the beautiful white doves scattered across the top.

Acknowledgements

I now have a group of people who never want to see my name pop up in their inbox again because of how many revisions I had for this book. To Ruth, John, Marissa, and April: I owe you a hundred times over for your thoughtful input, kind words and most of all, your patience. Please unblock me from your contact list until it's time to edit the next one.

To my big sister Kim, we've been together through all of life's hardest moments and it sure is fun to finally share the good ones with you, too.

Cash, although mine are the only fiction books you read, your contributions to my proofreading and editing process are immeasurable. Thank you for being there for me when I need it most.

To Rachel, thank you for letting me use your potential baby's name for my character. Good thing she didn't end up murdering anyone, eh?

To the people who have become my best friends throughout each phase of my life, I can't thank you enough for your love and support. Mal, Brit, Ash, Heath, The JAK, and Pam – you make life more fun, and I wish I could see all of you a lot more often.

After Delta County came out, a lot of good things happened to me. The most important being reconnecting with my high school friends, who have supported me in every way this past year. To the girls of Delta County: I'll never be able to repay the kindness you've shown me, but I'll sure try.

To Jack Hirn, thank you for working so hard to change the life of a girl you've never met. I can't wait to see what happens next.

To my friends at Lively Beerworks in OKC, you have given me the best job I've ever had. I laugh every single day and get to meet the greatest people while also pouring the best beer in the state. I'm lucky to know you.

To Ty and Brandon with AllSweet in OKC, you've given me your friendship, your expertise, and let me use your beautiful studio. I can't wait to collaborate for years to come.

Haleigh and Marissa, thank you for carving out an entire afternoon to make sure I had the pictures I needed. I'd rather spend a day with you two than most anyone else.

To my extended family, who continue to support me even though I write murderous novels with foul language: thank you.

Finally, my biggest show of gratitude is always for the readers. Most of you don't know me and don't have any reason to support me the way you do. I wish you knew how much it means each time you buy one of my books, write a review, or send me a message telling me you enjoy my writing. A few minutes out of your day means the world to me. Your kindness has genuinely changed the way I look at this world.

If you'd like to reach out, find me on social media or e-mail me directly at info@jlhyde.com – I'd love to hear from you!

Made in the USA
Monee, IL
26 June 2024